David Schutte was born in Hornsey, North London. Brain surgeon, pop singer, and Olympic athlete are just some of the things he never achieved. He is now a financial adviser and specialist children's bookseller. He lives near Midhurst in West Sussex with his wife and children.

Wild Woods, Dark Secret is the third book in the Naitabal Mystery series. The other titles in the series are *Danger, Keep Out!*, *Wake Up, It's Midnight!* and *Behind Locked Doors.*

To Bobby

David

Schutte

×××××××
⊗ ⊗ ⊗

Also by David Schutte

Danger, Keep Out!
Wake Up, It's Midnight!
Behind Locked Doors

DAVID SCHUTTE

WILD WOODS, DARK SECRET

A Naitabal Mystery

To Bobby

Best Wishes

David Schutte

**MACMILLAN
CHILDREN'S BOOKS**

First published 1995 by Macmillan Children's Books

a division of Macmillan Publishers Limited
25 Eccleston Place London SW1W 9NF
and Basingstoke

Associated companies throughout the world

ISBN 0 330 33853 6

1 3 5 7 9 8 6 4 2

A CIP catalogue record for this book is available from the British
Library

Phottypeset by Intype, London
Printed by Mackays of Chatham PLC, Kent

TO

NANCI BERRY

with love and thanks

NAITABAL:	A wild species of human, aged about ten.
NAITABAL GRUNT:	Primitive Naitabal response used mainly on adults.
NAITABAL TORCH:	An electric torch with three colours, usually white, red and green.
NAITABAL MORSE:	A secret signalling code that cannot be deciphered by enemies or adults.
NAITAGONIA:	Any foreign soil in England occupied by Naitabals.

Rules for speaking Naitabal language

Words beginning with A: add "ang" to the end.

e.g. apple = *apple-ang*. The word "a", however, is just *ang*.

Words beginning with B, C or D: move the first letter to the end of the word, then add "ang" to the end.

e.g. banana = *anana-bang*; catapult = *atapult-cang*; disaster = *isaster-dang*.

Words beginning with E: add "eng" to the end.

e.g. elephant = *elephant-eng*.

Words beginning with F, G or H: move the first letter to the end of the word, then add "eng" to the end.

e.g. fool = *ool-feng*; groan = *roan-geng*; help = *elp-heng*.

Words beginning with I: add "ing" to the end.

e.g. ink = *ink-ing*. The word "I", however, is just *Ing*.

Words beginning with J, K, L, M or N: move the first letter to the end of the word, then add "ing" to the end.

e.g. jump = *ump-jing*; kill = *ill-king*; laugh = *augh-ling*; measles = *easles-ming*; night = *ight-ning*.

Words beginning with O: add "ong" to the end.

e.g. orange = *orange-ong*.

Words beginning with P, Q, R, S or T: move the first letter to the end of the word, then add "ong" to the end.

e.g. parrot = *arrot-pong*; queen = *een-quong* (notice that "qu" stays together); rabbit = *abbit-rong*; sausage = *ausage-song*; tickle = *ickle-tong*.

Words beginning with U: add "ung" to the end.

e.g. under = *under-ung*.

Words beginning with V, W, X, Y or Z: move the first letter to the end of the word, then add "ung" to the end.

e.g. vest = *est-vung*; witch = *itch-wung*; xylophone = *ylophone-xung*; young = *oung-yung*; zebra = *ebra-zung*.

For words beginning with CH, GH, PH, RH, SH, TH or WH, move the "H" with the first letter, but follow the "first letter" rules, as in:

chop = *op-chang*; ghost = *ost-gheng*; photo = *oto-phong*; rhesus = *esus-rhong*; shop = *op-shong*; thistle = *istle-thong*; why = *y-whung*.

For plurals, keep the "s" in the original position.

e.g. book = *ook-bang*; books = *ooks-bang*; pig = *ig-pong*; pigs = *igs-pong*.

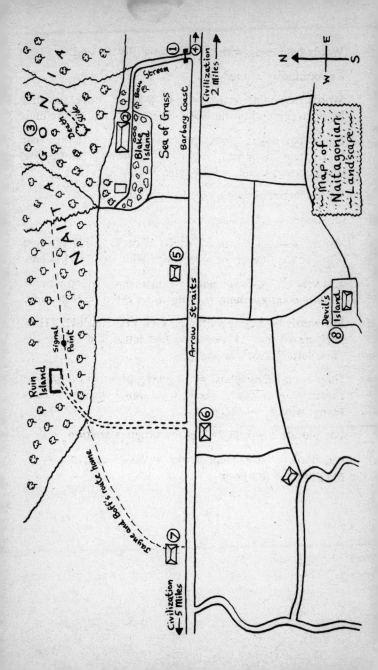

Contents

CHAPTER ONE

Naitabal Journey

"It's funny he didn't write to us," said Ben.

He was sitting in a corner of the train compartment, raising his voice in the hope that the other Naitabals could hear him. He obviously hadn't raised it high enough, because no one answered. Charlotte and Jayne, in spite of warning notices to the contrary, were leaning out of the windows on each side of the carriage. They were using their catapults to fire Naitabal acorns at passing telegraph poles, and shouting scores at each other.

"Thirty-six!" screamed Charlotte.

"Thirty-nine!" screamed Jayne.

Boff was in the far corner facing the engine. He was frowning and writing hieroglyphics on a big, lined pad. Two more seats were occupied by a pile of luggage. Above it, the luggage rack was occupied by a pile of Toby, who was asleep.

A small heap of bows and arrows, catapults and pea-shooters filled the last corner, still warm from recent, frenzied use. All the Naitabals were wearing Naitabal battledress, their faces streaked with mud to serve as camouflage. As camouflage, unfortunately, it was not doing its job. Every passenger on the train knew they were there. It was an old-style carriage with separate compartments, and the passengers in the adjacent ones were wishing they weren't and were praying for the journey to come to an end.

Ben raised his voice even louder – above the rattle of the wheels, above the wind, above the shouts of Jayne and Charlotte, and above the luggage rack, where he hoped it would pierce Toby's slumber.

"I said, *it's funny he didn't write to us*!" Ben shouted.

Jayne and Charlotte finished their game of Hit the Oncoming Telegraph Pole and closed the windows. Their scores were even, at thirty-nine each. Jayne's jet-black curls were blown to one side like a wind-sock, and Charlotte's hair looked like a mad hamster's nest. They used their fingers to rake themselves tidy and flopped on to the seats next to Ben.

"What did you say?" said Charlotte. "My ears are singing."

"I hope they've got a better voice than your mouth," mumbled Toby from the luggage rack. The sudden quiet had woken him up.

"My ears aren't singing exactly," said Jayne, "but the wind has made my face go numb."

Boff looked up from his book.

"You shouldn't have been leaning out of the windows in the first place," he said, peering through his glasses. "It's dangerous."

"All in a good cause," said Charlotte breathlessly. "We must have sown about a hundred Naitabal acorns along those embankments. Come back in ten years and count all the new oak trees."

Ben brought his voice down to its normal level and repeated his remark for the third time.

"I was saying, 'It's funny he didn't write to us.' "

"Do you mean Mr Blake?" said Charlotte, listening at last. "Of course he wrote to us – he wrote asking our

2

parents if we could go and stay with him."

"Yes," said Ben. "I know that."

Mr Blake was a cousin of Ben's neighbour, Miss Coates (known to the Naitabals as the old enemy battleship the SS *Coates*). When the Naitabals had solved his financial problems,* he had promised them the holiday of a lifetime.

"Our reward," said Jayne, "for finding his long-lost money."

"Yes," said Ben, with great patience, "I know that as well."

"What I thought was funny," Charlotte went on, "was how Mr Blake came down that night and had a secret meeting with our parents and the SS *Coates* and Mr Elliott. Didn't you think that was funny?"

Mr Elliott was Boff's neighbour. He was the builder who had built their tree-house for them in his garden, and he and Mr Blake had been childhood friends.

"Yes," said Jayne. "My parents were worried about me going at first – especially as I'm the youngest. But Mr Elliott and the SS *Coates* must have said nice things about Mr Blake and made it OK."

"Mr Blake sent a man to take my photo," muttered Toby. "But he didn't take pictures of any of you. That's what *I* thought was funny."

"Perhaps he couldn't remember what you looked like," said Jayne, unkindly.

"That's not what *I'm* talking about," said Ben. "You've all forgotten the important bit."

"Well, it was such a rush," Charlotte said. "With my family just getting back from holiday and unpacking and

*See *Danger, Keep Out!*

getting everything clean, and packing for this one, I didn't really have much time."

"I bet your mum did most of it," Toby murmured.

"She didn't!" said Charlotte, sending a few meaningful daggers towards Toby's slumbering form. "Just because your mum does everything for you, doesn't mean—"

"All right, all right," said Ben. "What I'm trying to *say* is, he didn't *write* to us."

"Explain," said Charlotte imperiously.

"Mr Blake said the holiday would be a sort of treasure hunt, didn't he? He said he'd send us the first clue."

"So he did! I'd forgotten about the clue."

"Well, he didn't write, so we haven't got it."

"He'll give it to us when we get there," said Jayne, shrugging. "Simple."

"That's not the point," said Ben. "If he'd sent it, we could have been trying to work it out on the journey."

"I phoned him yesterday," said Boff, looking up and then looking down again. "When it hadn't come I phoned several times, but there was no answer."

"He must have been out," said Jayne, stating the obvious.

"Oh, well," Ben shrugged. "He'll just have to tell us the first clue when we arrive, won't he?"

Charlotte suddenly groaned.

"I'm going to miss our tree-house," she said.

"Me, too," said Jayne.

"At least you've all slept in it recently," Charlotte went on. "But I haven't slept in it for two *weeks*. That's the trouble with going on holiday. However nice the beach is, you still have to spend the nights in a boring old house or a boring old ordinary old hotel with boring old ordinary *beds*!"

"Mr Blake's house is big," said Ben. "I bet it's so big

4

we get lost in it. And I bet it won't be boring with Mr Blake – he'll let us do anything we want."

"He might let us sleep in the garden," said Jayne, cheering up.

Above them, Toby turned over.

"I wish they'd make these luggage racks more comfortable," he complained. "I'm getting bruises."

"I don't know if you realize, Toby," Charlotte said, "but they weren't actually designed to be *slept* in. I know it looks like a hammock, but it isn't. Anyway, if you come down, we can put the rest of our bags up and have a bit more leg room."

Toby stirred into a crouching position and eased himself down over the side.

"Well, I think they *ought* to be designed to be slept in. They could be much comfier than sitting bolt upright in these hard seats."

"Yes, Toby."

Everyone knew it was just another of Toby's excuses for getting more sleep.

"They could sling about four hammocks between the luggage racks," he went on, "and there'd still be room for all the luggage *and* for everyone else to sit down. I think I'll write to the railways and suggest it. They'd get at least four more people in each compartment. *And* they'd be more comfortable."

"Anyway, I'm glad you're down," said Jayne. "There's another station soon, and the guards might see you."

But Toby's idea had started Ben on one of his favourite hobbies.

"I wonder what it would be like . . ." Ben began.

"Oh-oh, here we go," the others groaned, and even Boff looked up again from his notepad.

". . . if you had a really BIG hammock."

"You'd get lost in it."

"No, I mean a hammock tied between trees that were miles apart."

"They'd have to be pretty tall trees," said Toby, "otherwise the ropes would sag to the ground as soon as you got in."

"No, but just suppose they were tall trees – like those big ones in America – the giant something-or-others . . ."

"Sequoias," said Boff, absently.

"That's the ones," said Ben. "They're about three hundred metres high. Well, if you chose two that were about half a mile apart, and fixed the hammock to the top of each one, you could sleep about a hundred metres off the ground."

"How would you get in?" said Charlotte.

"A ladder?"

"Don't be stupid. What could it lean against? You couldn't lean it against the hammock. It would just fall over."

"And you couldn't get a ladder long enough, anyway," said Toby. "At least, not in our DIY store."

"I know," said Jayne. "You'd have to climb to the top of one of the trees and slide down the rope to the hammock."

"That's it," said Ben, glad that someone had seen sense at last. "And once you were in it you could start swinging from side to side. Think of it! Each swing would be hundreds of metres wide!"

"You'd go really fast," said Charlotte.

"How'd you get out?" said Toby.

"Parachute," said Charlotte promptly.

"I wouldn't like to be in it if there was a gale," said Jayne.

"Coo, I would!" said Ben. "That'd be the most fun. If

6

the wind was really hard, it might keep you blown out to one side for ages. Then, when the wind dropped, you'd come whizzing down again like a roller coaster!"

"It'd be much easier to make a huge swing," said Boff, joining in at last. "If you made the posts that held it half a mile high, you could swing a mile in each direction."

The other Naitabals considered this prospect with awe.

"Wow!"

"Think of it!"

"I wonder how fast you'd be going as you came whizzing back towards the bottom?" said Toby.

"And what if the posts were *ten* miles high," said Ben. "What then?"

Eventually, the exaggerations made the posts so high that the upswing was launching the Naitabals into space.

From there it was a short step to Ben wondering what the journey would be like if the train could travel at the speed of light.

"If this train could travel at the speed of light," Boff said, looking up again, "we'd get there in a thousandth of a second."

"We wouldn't need seats or hammocks," said Jayne. "There wouldn't be time to sit down."

"Even Toby wouldn't have time to go to sleep," said Charlotte. Then she looked at him and added, "Oh, I don't know, though."

"We wouldn't get there alive, of course," said Boff. "The acceleration would make us as flat as sheets of paper."

"It wouldn't me," said Ben. "I'd wear a suit of armour."

"It'd flatten that as well," said Boff. "You'd finish up inside it like a thin tin of sardines."

"At least we'd have something to eat when we got there," said Charlotte. "A nice Ben sandwich."

"You wouldn't be able to eat anything," said Jayne. "For one thing you'd be flat, and for another you'd be dead."

"What if the train went at the speed of sound, then?" said Ben. "How long would it take then?"

Boff pulled out his calculator.

"About fifteen minutes," he said.

"Toby would have time for a quick snooze," said Jayne.

"And if we put his head out of the window," said Charlotte, "we'd be going faster than his snores. We wouldn't hear a thing."

They were brought back to earth when they realized that the train was slowing down for the next station.

"Action STATION!" shouted Ben, and they all swung into their well-rehearsed routine. They dumped their luggage on to the seats, started dancing round, and made as much noise as possible. As they drew into the platform, they pulled their muddy faces into horrible contortions at the windows. It had worked at all the previous stops, and it worked like magic now. An elderly gentleman, who had been making steadily for their door, saw them and swerved to avoid it at the last moment. A young mother, noticing the unsavoury contents of their compartment, pointed and said to her small child, "That's what you'll grow up like if you don't eat your cabbage!" and whisked him away to safety.

By the time the train moved off, the Naitabals still had the compartment to themselves.

"Hooray!" grinned Ben. "It worked again!"

They tidied up, putting the strewn weapons back into the belts of their Naitabal battledress, and generally prepared themselves for the next stop, which was where they got off.

"I wonder what Cedric and the Igmopong are doing?" said Jayne.

Cedric Morgan lived next door to Charlotte. He was the leader of the rival gang, known to the Naitabals as the Igmopong.

"Does anyone care?" mumbled Toby.

"Probably trying to find a way into the Naitabal hut," said Ben.

"They've got no chance." Charlotte thought half longingly of the huge Naitabal oak. "They could borrow a ladder, but even if they made it to the hut they'd find it locked. Even Cedric wouldn't go so far as breaking a window."

"He might go up to our crow's nest," said Ben.

Charlotte laughed.

"Cedric? He's too scared of heights to go up *that* far."

There was a brief silence, then Jayne said, "No – but it's the first time that *none* of us have been there to stop him. I'm worried – with so much free time on his hands . . . I wonder what he *is* doing?"

CHAPTER TWO

The Missing Letter

The postman paused by the big yellow skip that blocked the entrance to Mr Elliott's front garden and scratched his head. He looked at the envelope in his hand for the umpteenth time. On the front it said "URGENT", and it was addressed:

> *The Naitabals*
> *The Naitabal Tree-House*
> *The Naitabal Oak*
> *Mr Elliott's Garden*
> *Brunswick Road*

The postman continued scratching his head. It was funny. He'd been curious about this one ever since it turned up at the sorting office at five o'clock that morning. He'd never had to deliver a letter to a tree-house before. They never mentioned tree-houses on the training course, and there was certainly nothing about them in the rule book. He'd checked. And when he'd asked his new mates, they'd just laughed.

His eyes travelled from the envelope to the big sign that was nailed to the old lilac tree next to the skip:

He noticed it every time he passed, particularly as the "Keep Out" was written in ghastly red paint that looked like blood dripping down. He'd often wondered exactly what a Naitabal was.

He made up his mind at last, climbed over the debris that overflowed from the skip, then picked his way carefully down the winding path towards the bottom of Mr Elliott's garden, stepping over strange objects as he went. He stood for a few seconds admiring the magnificent tree-house that sat astride the branches of Mr Elliott's enormous oak tree. Then he called out.

"Ahoy there! Anybody home?"

He watched the windows. Nothing appeared, and there was complete silence. He looked for a bell or a knocker. Most of the houses he delivered to had a bell or a knocker. Even if they didn't, at least they had a letterbox. This tree-house had no knocker and no letterbox. But – he suddenly noticed, if he craned his neck enough – it did have a bell. It was hanging underneath the hut two metres above his head, completely out of reach.

"That's a lot of use," he complained to himself. "How am I supposed to ring that?" He shouted *"Ahoy there!"*

again, louder this time. "Any Naitabals at home?" He half expected Naitabals to be some sort of strange animal. He hoped they didn't bite, whatever they were.

There was still no reaction, so he spoke to the letter.

"Where am I supposed to leave you, then?" he said. He waved it up and down as if trying to get an answer out of it.

When a squeaky voice said, "They're not in!" the postman nearly jumped out of his uniform. He stared at the envelope.

"Well, wrap me up and send me parcel post!" he said. "A talking letter!" He spoke to it confidentially while secretly glancing around for the real owner of the voice. "Keep talking like that, my fine envelope, and you'll make me a fortune!"

"I can take it, if you want."

"What? Take my fortune, when I've only just made it?"

"No! The letter! I can take the letter!"

The postman half wished letters *could* talk. It would make his job a lot easier sometimes.

"I'm up here."

He looked in the direction of the latest squeak and saw a fat-faced boy up a tree in the next-door garden. The boy was standing in the ruins of a tree-house that looked as if it had been charged by a flying rhinoceros. The postman recognized him. He hadn't had his postman's job for long, but Cedric Morgan was already known to him as one of the trouble-makers of the neighbourhood.

"You're not a Naitabal, are you?"

Cedric pulled a face.

"Pooh! I wouldn't want to be a grotty Naitabal in a hundred billion years!"

12

"Well, I can't give you the letter, then."

Cedric suddenly realized that this sweeping condemnation of his sworn enemies might have been too hasty. He was hoping to get the letter and steam it open before the Naitabals got back. It was bound to be a secret letter, and the more he learned about Naitabal secrets, the easier it would be to plot against them.

It was Cedric's dearest wish to own their superior treehouse, even for a day, and he was constantly thinking up plans to get it, legally or illegally – he didn't much care which.

"I can still take it for them," he said. "They'll be back soon, and it'll save you a lot of trouble if I do take it, won't it?"

"Ah!" said the postman. "But how will I know you've given it to them?"

"I will – honest. You can ask them tomorrow."

"Cross your heart?"

"Yep," said Cedric. He crossed his fingers behind his back and used the other hand to cross his heart. Cedric believed that crossing his fingers behind his back cancelled out promises. It meant he could lie and cheat as much as he liked. Cedric crossed his fingers a lot.

"And hope to die?"

"Of course," said Cedric. He couldn't see the point of crossing his heart and not hoping to die.

"And now," said the postman (a novice at delivering letters, but an expert on hands hidden behind backs), "say it while I can see both of your hands spread out in front of you."

"W-what?"

"Come on, let's see those hands."

Reluctantly, Cedric spread his palms where the postman could see them.

13

"Now say it – 'Cross my heart and hope to die'."

Cedric started to say "Cross my heart . . ." as he carefully crossed one ankle across the other. Ankles were just as good. Better than fingers, in fact – much more powerful. ". . . And hope to die," he finished.

The postman studied him briefly, then said, "No. You had your legs crossed."

"I didn't."

"You did. I saw 'em."

"All right." Cedric wondered if crossing his eyes would count, and whether the postman would notice at that distance. His only worry was that if he crossed his eyes he might fall out of the tree. "I'll say it again with them uncrossed."

"Sorry, mate. You had your chance. I'll take it to Charlotte's house instead. She must know them Naitabals, I reckon. I've seen her down here a few times."

Cedric wanted the letter badly, and his brain worked at lightning speed to think how he could get it. Charlotte's house was next door to his on the other side. He could get there quicker than the postman, who would be hampered by the mounds of rubbish in Mr Elliott's garden.

Cedric vacated his tree at speed. A slight splintering sound and a brief cry of pain were soon followed by his footsteps thudding on the grass towards his house. He ran up to his bedroom, changed his red jumper to a green one, grabbed the rubber dinosaur head from his bed, and dashed out to the front before the postman appeared on the road.

The postman had been further delayed by the sight of a rusty old tin can on Mr Elliott's path. It was years since he'd kicked a rusty old tin can, and the thought of it was making the muscles in his right leg twitch. He glanced

14

round. He couldn't see anyone watching from any windows, and he might never have a better opportunity. He took a run at it, felt the lovely twang as it connected with his shoe, and watched with great satisfaction as it soared in a perfect arc and landed in the skip.

"Goal!" he shouted, forgetting himself. He glanced round again nervously, straightened his uniform, and brushed a patch of rust from the tip of his shoe. He climbed over the remaining obstacles as if nothing unusual had happened and emerged into Brunswick Road. He strode past Cedric's house and turned in at Charlotte's gate, still clutching the envelope. He pulled up short when he found that the path was blocked by a small dinosaur wearing a green jumper.

"Is that for us?" said a high-pitched voice from inside the head. It pointed at the letter with a suspiciously human-looking finger.

"It is. It's for the Naitabals, really, but there's no one in, so I'm delivering it to Charlotte's house. Is she in?"

"Yes," said the muffled, squeaky voice.

The postman knocked on the triceratops' middle horn.

"Is that Charlotte in there?"

"Yes," said the squeak.

He handed the letter over, along with some others. The hand grabbed them – rather roughly for Charlotte, the postman thought. Then he strode on down the road, mission accomplished.

He didn't turn back. He didn't see the dinosaur cram all but one of the letters into Charlotte's letterbox. He didn't see it stuff the last one up its rather human shirt. Neither did he see the dinosaur snatch its head off to become Cedric again as it hopped back over the low wall that separated the gardens.

Neither did he see Charlotte's seven-year-old brother, Harry, watching from an upstairs window.

Cedric threw the triceratops headpiece into the sitting room and sneaked into his kitchen. He could hear the vacuum cleaner upstairs, which meant his mother was out of the way. He filled the electric kettle, plugged it in and switched it on.

He wanted to see what was in that letter, and he wanted to see quick. (He didn't know yet that all the Naitabals were away for a whole week or more.)

He stood at the kitchen door, listening. The kettle seemed to be taking ages. The vacuum cleaner went off and Cedric stiffened. It started up again, and he breathed a sigh of relief. Still the kettle wasn't doing anything. He'd switched it on, hadn't he? He checked. Yes, he had. He'd plugged it in, hadn't he? Yes, he had. The socket on the wall was switched on, wasn't it? He checked. No, it wasn't – no wonder the stupid thing wasn't boiling.

At the same time as he flipped the switch, the vacuum cleaner went off again upstairs, and he heard its little wheels squeaking on the carpet above him. He held his breath. The kettle started making its loud rushing noises as he eagerly fingered the envelope. Any minute now he'd know who was writing to the Naitabals, and what secrets they were hiding. Steam was beginning to drift out of the kettle's spout. He held the gummed flap over it, half expecting to see it pop open like magic, but it didn't. Now the kettle was making a lot of noise and bumping and thumping and he kept the envelope in the steam.

"What are you doing, darling?"

16

His mother had appeared in the doorway behind him, and Cedric was so shocked he leapt from the kitchen floor like an Apollo rocket. As he descended earthwards again he whipped the letter up his jumper, hoping she hadn't seen it. He turned.

"I – " His brain, such as it was, was working double time. "I – I was just making you a nice cup of coffee, Mum."

Mrs Morgan smiled and looked at him lovingly.

"You're such a sweet boy, Cedric, darling. Let Mummy hug you."

Before he could escape, she came across and buried his plump face in her mountainous landscape. She started patting his head rhythmically, but sensed that he wasn't comfortable. She discovered his arm between them, clutching his stomach.

"Are you feeling all right, love?" she said, drawing back.

"Yes, thanks. Why?"

"I just wondered why you were holding your stomach, dear . . . And why you've gone all stiff."

Cedric pulled away.

"Just hungry, Mum, that's all." He rubbed his stomach as he said it, but stopped when it started to make a tell-tale rustling noise. "Shall I bring your coffee up?"

"That'll be nice, dear."

"Where'll you be?"

"In the bedroom. I just came down for a duster."

She disappeared and Cedric switched on the kettle again. He extracted the letter and held it over the spout. Steam issued copiously for a few seconds as the water boiled, but then settled down to a gentle mist as the kettle turned itself off. Cedric pressed the switch several times, but now it wouldn't stay down.

17

He removed the envelope and examined it. Apart from getting hot, nothing seemed to have happened to it at all. It was still gummed as firmly as before, and the whole operation was proving far less simple than he'd imagined.

He had another idea and took the lid off the kettle, nearly scalding himself in the process. He threw the envelope gum side down on to the steaming cauldron and watched as it started to sag in the middle.

"*I'll take my coffee up with me.*"

This time Cedric jumped higher than a ballet dancer with a thistle in his tights. While he was still in mid-air he realized he wasn't going to come down quick enough to hide the letter.

"What's that letter doing on the kettle, Cedric? I thought you were making me a cup of coffee?"

Cedric looked at the letter and the kettle as if he'd never seen them before in his life. He flicked the letter off, retrieved it from where it landed, and dropped it again as it burnt his fingers.

"You weren't trying to steam it open, by any chance?"

"I – I've written a letter to Ben Tuffin and Charlotte and the others," Cedric blurted out. He said it all in one breath and got quicker and quicker as he started to run out of oxygen, "and-I-wanted-to-say-something-else-so-I-was-trying-to-steam-it-open-and-write-it-and-stick-it-down-again."

"Well, you silly darling. Just write it on the outside."

"Eh?"

Mrs Morgan, meaning business, had advanced and picked up the letter. "Just write the other thing you wanted to say on the back." She grabbed a pen and was already hovering it over the back of the envelope. Luckily, the letter had fallen face down and she hadn't seen the stamps and the postmark.

18

"Can't you do it in pencil?" said Cedric, with desperation creeping into his voice.

She ignored him.

"I've got the pen now, dear. What did you want to write?"

Cedric knew his mother's businesslike moods. There was no way out, and she wouldn't be satisfied until she'd written his message on the back of the envelope.

"Er – 'See you soon' please."

" 'See you soon'?"

"Yes. 'See you soon.' "

"That's what you were steaming the letter open for – to say 'See you soon'?"

"Yes."

Mrs Morgan's landscape heaved up and down as her quick hand wrote the message. Cedric was horrified as he saw her adding the fatal, tell-tale words, "from Cedric".

"There you are," she said, handing it back to him. "Simple. And when you've made my coffee you can deliver it, can't you?"

Five minutes later, Cedric was in his ramshackle treehouse. Now that his name had been written on the back of the envelope there was no way he could give it to the Naitabals. He ripped it open. Inside was a single sheet of paper folded in half, and on it were the words:

> *Take the taxi to the gate.*
> *Ring the bell, stand and wait.*
> *From the place where Elliott miaowed,*
> *East to the tree that touches a cloud.*

Cedric's eyes bulged as he drank the words hungrily, and slowly unbulged as he read it for the second and third time.

His expression changed to a sneer. He pushed the letter back into the torn envelope, screwed the whole thing up and tossed it to the ground below.

"Pooh!" he said. "Just a load of rubbish."

Next door, Harry's head sank down behind the fence.

CHAPTER THREE

Naitabal Morse

"Never mind what Cedric's doing," said Charlotte. She turned to Boff, who was still buried deep in his notepad. "What I want to know is, what's Boff doing? His pencil's been working overtime the whole journey."

Boff looked up, squinting through his glasses.

"Can you keep a secret?" he said.

"What do you mean," Charlotte exploded, "*can I keep a secret*? Of course I c—"

"Only joking," said Boff calmly, watching Charlotte boiling over.

"You—!"

"What I've been doing," Boff explained, "is designing Naitabal Morse."

"What?"

Suddenly everyone was paying attention. Anything new from Boff was usually worth listening to.

"The trouble with ordinary Morse code," Boff continued, "is that all the dots and dashes are too difficult to learn. I mean, everyone knows how to send SOS in Morse, but—"

"I don't," admitted Toby.

"You must do. Everyone should know that."

"Well, I don't. I've never been taught it. I mean, it's not something we're born knowing, is it?"

"You can learn it now, then," said Boff.

"I know it's got dots and dashes in it," – vaguely – "somewhere."

Jayne and Charlotte giggled.

"Toby! Morse code's all dots and dashes!"

Boff soldiered on through the sound barrier.

"SOS is dot-dot-dot, dash-dash-dash, dot-dot-dot."

"That means," said Jayne, making sure Toby understood, "if you've got a torch, you do three short flashes, then three long flashes, then three short ones again. Dots are quick flashes, and dashes are long ones."

"I might get mixed up, though. I might think it's dash-dash-dash, dot-dot-dot, dash-dash-dash."

Charlotte had the answer.

"Think of the dots as coins, and the dashes as matchsticks," she suggested. "That's how I do it. Then all you've got to remember is that SOS is worth *more money than matches*."

"That's good," admitted Toby. "Even I can remember that."

"Good," said Boff. "You might be glad some day."

"I tried learning Morse code once," said Ben. "But I kept forgetting. I could only remember about ten letters at a time, and if I learnt another ten, I'd forget the first ten."

"There's not much point learning it, anyway," Boff went on.

"Why not?" said Charlotte.

"Because of the other problem."

"What other problem?"

"Well, if we signal to each other in Morse code at night, other people can see the flashing—"

"Like the Igmopong . . .?"

" – Yes – or parents – and if they know Morse code

they can work out what we're saying to each other."

"We could do Morse in Naitabal language," suggested Jayne.

"That'd be better than nothing," admitted Boff. "But the Igmopong could even work that out if they wrote it down. It confuses them when we speak it, but . . ."

"So what's the answer?" said Charlotte. "Have you thought of something else?"

"Yes," said Boff. "*Naitabal* Morse."

The others had been watching him for days now, at odd moments drawing squiggles and dots on pieces of paper. They had wondered what he was up to, but it was never any use asking Boff until he'd finished working things out. Now they realized.

"If I tried to teach you ordinary Morse code," Boff continued, "and I told you that 'A' was dot-dash, 'B' was dash-dot-dot-dot, 'C' was dash-dot-dash-dot, 'D' was dash-dot-dot, 'E' was dot, and 'F' was dot-dot-dash-dot, you wouldn't remember much of it, would you?"

"I've remembered 'E'," said Toby. "It's dot."

Charlotte gave him one of her sideways glances.

"Well done, Toby," she said.

"But if I told you that in *Naitabal* Morse, 'A' was dot, 'B' was dot-dot, 'C' was dot-dot-dot, and 'D' was dot-dot-dot-dot, you'd remember it, wouldn't you?"

"Don't tell me," said Charlotte, using her fingers to start counting. " 'Z' is dot-dot-dot-dot-dot-dot-dot-dot-dot-dot-dot-dot-dot-dot-dot-dot-d—!"

"No, it isn't twenty-six dots, Charlotte. But you can all tell me what 'C' is, can't you?"

"Dot-dot-dot," said a chorus.

"But you can't tell me what it is in ordinary Morse, can you?"

The chorus fell apart, there were several guesses, but no one got it right.

"So," said Boff, "that means you're ready for the next bit."

He laid a piece of paper in front of them which looked something like this:

WHITE DOT	WHITE DASH	RED	GREEN	WHITE WIGGLE
A .	E -	I .	O .	U ~
B ..	F --	J ..	P ..	V ~~
C ...	G ---	K ...	Q ...	W ~~~
D	H ----	L	R	X ~~~~
		M	S	Y ~~~~~
		N	T	Z ~~~~~~

"Notice," he said, pointing, "that it's just like Naitabal language – split the alphabet into five sections, starting with the vowels."

"A, E, I, O and U," said Jayne helpfully.

"And then all you've got to remember," said Boff, "is dot, dash, red, green, wiggle."

"I can remember it, all right," said Ben. "Dot, dash, red, green, wiggle. But what does it mean?"

"Simple." Everything was simple to Boff.

The others stared as he reached into his rucksack, rummaged inside, then triumphantly held up a torch. They could see straight away that it wasn't just an ordinary torch – it was one that had something special about it.

"What you need," said Boff, "is a Naitabal torch."

They all crowded round as Boff showed it to them. It

could turn on and off like any other, with a button on top to do quick flashes (dots), or long flashes (dashes). But then he showed them why it was a Naitabal torch. On the front were two coloured filters, one red and one green. They could be slid across the glass to make the light red or green. He pulled the red filter across, and did one short flash.

"That's the letter 'I'," he said.

They all looked at the chart.

"One dot, red," said Jayne. "That's easy."

"What's this?" Boff changed the filter to green and flashed five times.

Another glance at the chart, and Ben said, "S."

"OK," said Toby. "Even I've got the red and the green, but what about the wiggle?"

"Wiggles are white," said Boff. He changed the torch back to white in a split second, then held it up. He switched it on and moved it horizontally from left to right in a big, generous movement, then back again. "There. A wiggle is just a big move from side to side. If you do it once, it's 'U'. If you do it six times, it's 'Z'."

The others were impressed. They'd only been learning for a few minutes, and they knew it already.

"Dot, dash, red, green, wiggle," chanted Jayne.

"Good," said Boff. "There's just one more thing, though."

"What?"

"What do you do if—"

". . . You haven't got a Naitabal torch with red and green lenses . . .?" Charlotte finished for him, because she'd just thought of it herself.

"Simple again," said Boff. With a quick grin and a flourish he turned his piece of paper over, and there on the back was another chart:

25

WHITE	WHITE	WHITE	WHITE	WHITE
DOT	DASH	UP	ROUND	WIGGLE
A .	E -	I |	O o	U ~
B ..	F --	J ||	P oo	V ~~
C ...	G ---	K |||	Q ooo	W ~~~
D	H ----	L ||||	R oooo	X ~~~~
		M |||||	S ooooo	Y ~~~~~
		N ||||||	T oooooo	Z ~~~~~~

"All you've got to remember for this one is dot, dash, up, round, wiggle."

"Dot, dash, up, round, wiggle," chanted the others. "That's easy as well."

Boff switched on the torch and did a big up/down movement.

"That's the letter 'I'," he said. "Up and down looks like an 'I' so you can't really forget which is which. And round – " he did a big circle with the torch – "is just like an 'O', so you can't really forget that, either."

"Hey!" said Toby suddenly, checking the chart. "SOS in Naitabal Morse is *all* money! Five rounds, one round, and five rounds."

"Unfortunately, it takes a long time to signal," said Boff. "So if you're in deep trouble, and you haven't got a Naitabal torch, you can use the ordinary SOS – dot-dot-dot, dash-dash-dash, dot-dot-dot."

"Even if you have got a Naitabal torch, it might take a while," said Charlotte. "Five greens, one green, and five greens again."

"That's why I've got a special SOS for Naitabal torches," said Boff. He turned his pad towards Charlotte so she could see where he'd written it. "SOS in Naitabal Morse is just red-green-red."

"IOI," said Toby, laughing.

26

Then Boff produced an even bigger surprise – he reached into his rucksack and held out four more Naitabal torches that were hidden inside, one for each of them. Everyone was so impressed with Boff's new idea, they split up into two teams, pulled down the blinds, and spent the rest of the journey signalling to each other across the compartment in Naitabal Morse. Half an hour later, they all knew it as if they'd known it all their lives.

The last message anyone had time to send was flashed out in a panic on Boff's torch. It said: "*Green, wiggle, green-green-green-green, green-green-green-green-green, green-green-green-green-green-green, dot, green-green-green-green-green-green, red, green, red-red-red-red-red-red.*"

"OUR STATION!" shouted Charlotte, and they all fell over each other as they scrambled for their luggage.

CHAPTER FOUR

See No Evil, Hear No Evil, Speak No English

The train drew to a halt. Boff opened the door and the five Naitabals stepped down on to the platform. They were in a new, strange place, and they were excited.

There were a few houses clustered round the station, but looking along the tracks in the distance they could see mostly hills and woods.

"This is a foreign country, really," whispered Ben as they hauled their luggage past an extremely English-looking man reading an obviously English newspaper. "We're from Naitagonia, and we don't speak English. That means we can't read any of the signs. And we don't understand what anyone says to us."

The others caught on to the idea immediately.

"And they can't understand anything we say, either," said Charlotte.

"Because we only talk Naitabal language," said Jayne.

"Naitagonian," corrected Ben.

They struggled along the platform towards the barrier, and from that moment switched to Naitabal language. They were all anxious to try out their new-found ignorance on the locals, who would be convinced that they were from some exotic far-off land.

"*Icket-tong arrier-bang,*" said Ben at last as they neared the ticket barrier.

The ticket collector, who had been watching them approaching, swept his gaze up and down their strange clothing, and eyed their weapons and mud-streaked faces with suspicion.

"Just escaped from the woods, have we?" he said, trying to be funny. Then he gave them an even stranger look as Jayne and Charlotte started conversing.

"*Ing on't-dang ink-thong e-heng understands-ung is-thong, o-dang ou-yung?*" said Charlotte.

"*O-ning ance-chang*, said Jayne.

"Tickets, please," said the man hastily.

"*Ardon-pong?*" said Ben.

"T-i-c-k-e-t-s," said the man slowly, deciding they must be foreigners. "Where – are – your – ti – ckets?" He held up the one he'd just collected from the person in front of them.

"*Ah-ang!*" exclaimed Ben. "*Icket-tong!*"

The girls started giggling as Ben spoke a stream of Naitabal language to Boff, and Boff produced the tickets.

"Thank you," said the ticket man.

"*Y-ming leasure-pong*," said Boff.

"*Asty-ning an-ming*," said Jayne suddenly, pointing.

They looked. On the far side of the barrier, a gruff-looking man was standing. He was holding a large piece of cardboard with the single word "NAITABALS" written on it, but he was whistling and trying to pretend that he and the notice had nothing to do with each other.

The Naitabals gravitated towards him, and as soon as he saw them he quickly lowered the card.

"Naitabals?" he said, relieved, and added, "Whatever Naitabals are supposed to be."

"*Ild-wung ildren-chang*," Ben scowled.

The man, who was evidently the taxi-driver sent to collect them, looked alarmed.

29

"Do you speak English?" he said, worried.

"*O-ning!*" said Ben, nodding.

The taxi-driver made two more attempts to get some sense out of them, then gave up and tried to take two of the heavier bags off Jayne and Charlotte. They immediately protested (in Naitabal language) that they were just as strong as boys any day. Why didn't he help Toby, who was in danger of going to sleep standing up? Or Ben, who'd brought six cases when everyone else had brought two?

A short argument followed. The taxi-driver didn't understand a single word the Naitabals said, and the Naitabals pretended not to understand a single word the taxi-driver said. As a result, there was glorious confusion. At the end of it, the taxi-driver carried nothing, and the Naitabals struggled along with their luggage, arms aching, laughing until their sides and jaws ached as well.

When they were ensconced in the enormous taxi, they resumed their conversation in Naitabal language, much to the added confusion of the taxi-driver. He was still wondering what Naitabals were, exactly, because he'd never heard of such people in his life.

"*Ister-ming Lake-bang ives-ling in-ing ang ansion-ming*," announced Jayne. *Mister Blake lives in a mansion.*

"*He doesn't*," said Toby. He spoke slowly in Naitabal language so that the others could keep up. "*It's just a big country house.*"

"*Mr Elliott said it was a mansion.*"

As the taxi started up and manoeuvred its way out of the station, everyone thought of Mr Elliott's house.

"*Anything's a mansion compared with Mr Elliott's house,*" Ben pointed out.

"*But Mr Blake's house is big, though. It's got nine bedrooms.*"

"*That's one each, and four left over,*" said Charlotte, keeping up the Naitabal language to confuse the taxi-driver.

They heard him murmuring to himself.

"Must be some of them East Europeans who used to be in the Soviet Union . . ."

"*It'd be much more fun if we could all sleep in one room and have eight left over,*" said Jayne. "*It'd be like sleeping in the Naitabal hut, then.*"

The taxi wound through the town and headed out into the countryside on a fast, winding road.

"What – country – do – you – come – from?" said the taxi-driver slowly. His curiosity had got the better of him.

Ben made a Naitabal grunt, which meant he wanted the taxi-driver to speak even more slowly. The question was repeated at painful length, and the driver's hands left the steering wheel as he made expansive gestures.

"*Ah-ang!*" grinned Ben. "*Naitagonia.*"

"Naitagonia?" repeated the driver, and there followed a tremendous cheer with noddings and laughter from his strange passengers.

"*I'm going to miss our tree-house,*" said Charlotte, keeping faithfully to Naitabal language. "*We've never been away from it together for more than a few days since Mr Elliott built it for us.*"

"*O-ning.*"

"*A week is going to be torture.*"

"*I hope Cedric doesn't get at it,*" said Ben.

"*He won't find out we've all gone until the end of next week,*" said Charlotte. "*Then it'll suddenly start dawning on his neolithic brain.*"

"*How much further is it?*" Boff asked the driver, but of course the driver didn't understand a word.

Boff gestured and pointed, and at last was understood.

"Only a mile or so now," said the driver, holding up one finger.

The Naitabals all pointed to their watches and started screaming with excitement like monkeys.

"*We could build a tree-house here*," said Ben.

"*If we tried to build one it'd probably look similar to Cedric's*," said Jayne.

"*As if it's been hit by a tycoon*," said Ben.

"*I think you mean 'typhoon'*," said Charlotte.

"*I don't*," said Ben. "*Some of those tycoons are big and fat.*"

"*I don't think our tree-house would look quite as bad as that*," said Toby. "*We'd make sure it wasn't.*"

Half a mile down a long straight piece of road, the taxi started slowing down. They were in the middle of a wide, flat valley, mostly decked with fields full of sheep. Five Naitabal heads were straining forwards and sideways, each one trying to be the first to catch a glimpse of Mr Blake's house. But the hedges that lined the road hid most of the view, and when they could see the hills that rose above the valley, they found most of the features were hidden by dense woodland.

The taxi was signalling right. It slowed down almost to a halt, then turned across the road and came to a standstill in front of a tall pair of pillars that supported huge wrought-iron gates. The gates were closed.

Ben pointed. Running from each side of the pillars was a high stone wall. On top of the wall, at least three metres high, there was broken glass embedded in mortar, all topped off with coils of barbed wire.

"*Are you sure this is the right place?*" Ben asked the driver in Naitabal language.

The driver eventually understood Ben's gestures and

indicated the ornate lettering that was welded into the pattern of the wrought-iron gates.

"Darkwood House," he read aloud, slowly. "That's where you wanted, wasn't it?"

"*Ah-ang!*" said a chorus of Naitabal voices. "*Ank-thong ou-yung!*"

They all got out and started unloading their luggage.

"Sorry – to – drop – you – at – the – gate," said the driver, slowly. "I – don't – suppose – you – can – understand – me – but – I've – strict – instructions – to – drop – you – at – the – gate." Then he gave up, and said quickly, half to himself, "He doesn't want anyone up there, not even the postman."

The Naitabals noticed the slot in the gates where a strong post-box had been welded on.

"I – leave – you – at – the – gate," he said again slowly, pointing, and the Naitabals grinned stupidly back.

All the luggage was out of the boot by this time. The driver waved them goodbye and turned to go back the way he had come.

The taxi headed back along the straight road towards the town and the driver reached across for the mobile telephone. He keyed a number rapidly and lifted the hand-set as the ringing tone sounded.

"Frank?"

"Yeah," said a voice at the other end.

"They've arrived."

"Good."

"They're a funny lot, though."

"What makes you say that?"

"They're Naitagonians."

"They're what?"

"Naitagonians. They're all dressed in Naitagonian costume, and not one of them speaks a word of English."

"No one said anything about that."

"Well, they're here now."

The taxi-driver replaced the receiver and his taxi sped on towards the town.

Toby was nearest the big bell-push on the left-hand pillar, and he leaned on it long and hard.

"That was fun," said Charlotte, relieved to speak English again. They all laughed as they remembered the looks that had appeared on the taxi-driver's face as they had bombarded him with Naitabal language.

They waited.

Ben went to the gates and pressed his face between the bars.

"Look," he said. "Everything behind this gate is Naitagonia. It's our homeland."

"Of course," said Charlotte. "That's why we can't understand anyone outside."

"The main road's as straight as an arrow," Ben added, turning. "It's the Arrow Straits."

"The drive is curved like a bow," said Jayne, pointing through the gates. "That must be Bow Street."

"It can't be Bow *Street*," said Boff.

"All right. Bow *Stream*, then."

"There's a real stream running next to it," said Toby, laughing his silent laugh. "Quiver River."

Everyone else laughed and looked at where Quiver River emerged through a narrow culvert under the gates and into the ditch that ran along the main road.

"In that case we should call those woods on the hill WigwamWoods," suggested Charlotte.

"That means all the trees must have squaw roots," said Toby, and got another laugh.

Then Boff said, "I'm not sure about 'Wigwam Woods'. How about the Sea of Trees?"

"That's a good idea," said Jayne. "Especially as it *is* a sea of trees."

"No," said Ben firmly. "It's just Naitagonia."

The gates still hadn't opened, and Ben jostled Toby away from the bell.

"All we want now," he said, pressing it himself, "is a Sea of Gates Opening."

While Ben leaned on the bell, Darkwood House became Blake Island, the large meadow embraced by Bow Stream became the Bay of Grass, and the barbed-wire-topped walls and fences that defended the property became the Barbary Coast.

"You have to cross the Barbary Coast to get in," concluded Ben, pressing the bell yet again.

"I'll draw a map later," said Charlotte.

Still nothing had happened to the gates, so Boff had a try at pushing the bell, followed by Jayne, then Charlotte. When all efforts had failed, Ben decided to lean on the bell permanently. If there was anyone at the other end of the wire, they'd be driven mad.

They discussed this first hitch in the arrangements.

"What do we do now?" said Jayne.

"Climb over," said Toby.

"Have you looked on top of the gates and on top of the wall?" said Charlotte. "The Barbary Coast?"

Toby looked up at the barbed wire and broken glass and screwed up his face in a thoughtful silence. Then they all had a turn at pushing and pulling the gates. Boff applied a little more brainpower than the others. He looked closely at how the gates were hung, then eased them sideways into the walls without any resistance at all.

"*Imple-song!*" he announced, pleased with himself. The others felt like fools and made loud donkey noises.

Much relieved, they picked up their luggage and moved with it through the gap that Boff had created.

"It's got an electronic lock," said Boff. "It's just not connected. You would have thought the gates would open automatically if they were unlocked. Something must be broken."

"It's funny we didn't hear it unlock," said Charlotte.

"Perhaps it was unlocked ready for us coming," said Ben.

"Better close them again," said Jayne, pushing them together. "At least they look locked to anyone passing by."

At last they turned their attention to Bow Stream, the long tarmac drive that swept up towards the wooded hillside in front of them. Two minutes of walking, half carrying, half dragging their bags, brought them to a sharp turn to the left. There were trees on both sides of them now, and the drive climbed higher and higher. Jayne pointed.

"Look!"

Some distance ahead of them, emerging from the trees as they walked, was a huge white house.

"Blake Island!" said Charlotte.

They all turned to enjoy the view that opened out on their left. They could see right across the broad, flat valley bottom to the hills that climbed the other side. There were a few isolated farmhouses, a distant church spire, and mountains beyond the hills on the distant skyline.

"What a wonderful place!" said Jayne.

They walked on, and eventually reached Darkwood House itself. As they approached they could hear loud music from a radio. The front door was wide open.

Boff rang the big bell, and when there was no answer, he said, "Something's not right."

The man with blond hair put down the telephone and walked to the window that overlooked the valley. He picked up a pair of binoculars and held them to his eyes, focusing them on the big white house that lay nearly a mile away on the opposite hillside.

"Anything?" said the other voice in the room. It belonged to a pint-size little man with broad rounded shoulders and short-cropped hair.

"No sign of Blake, but the kids are there, all right. Odd-looking bunch. Talk about primitive." He lowered the binoculars. "Jack says they can't speak any English."

"Really? First I've heard."

"At least they shouldn't be any trouble. I mean, if they find anything, they won't be able to tell anyone."

"True. Seems a bit pointless, though."

"Unless there's some advanced brain in the cop shop who speaks this – what was it Jack said? – Naitagonian."

"Oh, yes. Highly likely."

The blond raised the binoculars again. Five minutes later, he spoke.

"They've reached the front door. It's already open, but they're not going in. Oh – yes they are. They've gone in. Still no sign of Blake, though."

"All we've got to do now," said the little man, "is wait until our little foreign visitors have gone to sleep. What do you reckon? About eleven?"

"No. They'll be excited. Unable to sleep. Perhaps a bit later?"

"Yeah. A bit later should do nicely."

"I don't know why you're worrying," said Charlotte. "Mr Blake's probably just popped into town for something."

"But his car's in the yard," said Jayne. "He must be here somewhere."

"Perhaps he walked into town," said Ben, "and left the entrance gates open in case we got here first."

"And the radio playing . . ." said Boff.

"Come on," said Ben, "let's go in. We are invited, after all."

They went in. They passed a huge drawing room on the left, where the radio was blaring, and a huge dining room on the right. They stacked their luggage in the hall and went through to the back of the house, where they found the kitchen. There was a half-eaten meal on the table, including half a cup of cold tea.

"It's like the *Marie Celeste*," said Charlotte, shivering.

"What's the *Marie Celeste*?" said Jayne.

"It was a ship – over a hundred years ago – an old sailing ship. The crew of another ship saw it drifting on the ocean, and when they boarded it they found that all the crew were missing. The tables had half-eaten meals on them as if the sailors had seen something terrible and jumped overboard."

"There's a note," said Jayne, moving forward. She scooped up a piece of paper that was lying on the table, pinned down by a salt cellar. As she read it, a strange look came over her face.

"This is weird," she said in a quiet voice. "Very weird."

The way she said it was enough to get the others

interested. They crowded round her, trying to look, but Jayne kept a tight grip on it and insisted on reading it aloud.

"*Dear Miss Coates,*" she read slowly, "*I've had to go away for a few days. Please feed the cat. His name is Elliott, and he spends most of his time in the woods. Thank you. Charles Blake.*"

CHAPTER FIVE

Where is Mr Blake?

The other Naitabals agreed with Jayne that weird was the only word to describe the note – extremely weird. The weirdest thing was the names. Miss Coates, of course, was Ben's next-door neighbour back home, and Mr Blake's cousin. And Mr Elliott was Boff's next-door neighbour – not a cat at all.

The Naitabals read the note to themselves and to each other several times.

"It still doesn't make any sense," Ben proclaimed, when they'd all had their fill. "Mr Blake knows we wouldn't let Miss Coates come with us in a million years. Even if we did, he'd be calling her *Edith*, wouldn't he, not 'Miss Coates'?"

The others agreed, and Charlotte added, "And it's a bit strange if he happens to have a cat called Elliott as well."

"Well," said Boff hesitantly, "that's not impossible. We know Mr Blake and Mr Elliott were childhood friends. Perhaps he called his cat 'Elliott' for a joke."

"That's true," said Ben. Then, suddenly realizing, "Mr Elliott calls his cockerel *Charles*, doesn't he? That's Mr Blake's first name! It *could* be a joke between them."

That part sounded plausible, but no one was a hundred per cent convinced about the "Dear Miss Coates".

"There can't be someone else up here called Miss Coates, can there?" Jayne said.

"There could be, of course," said Charlotte. "It just seems too much of a coincidence, that's all."

"And he knew we were coming," Jayne complained, beginning to feel cross. "He invited us! He wouldn't just get up in the middle of breakfast and go away for three days without warning us."

"And leave us to do the washing up," said Toby.

"Anyway," Jayne added, "why didn't he leave a note for *us*?"

"Perhaps he did," said Toby.

A brief search of the kitchen, however, revealed nothing of the kind. They pondered the problem a little longer, then Boff said suddenly, "Let's check the rest of the house."

"I'm starving," said Toby. "Can't we have some food first?"

"Oh, sure," said Charlotte. "And meanwhile Mr Blake might be lying upstairs unconscious."

Toby grabbed a piece of cold, stale toast from the rack, murmured, "I'll be able to carry him down better if I've had some grub," and followed the others up the stairs.

There were five double bedrooms, all at the front of the house, four of them with twin beds, and three of those with en suite bathrooms. At the back were four single rooms and two more bathrooms. All the rooms led off one long corridor that ran the length of the house through its middle. Every bed was made up ready, but there was no sign of any human beings to occupy them.

The Naitabals trooped downstairs. At the back of the house they discovered the most interesting room of all. It overlooked a wide yard on the far side. In it was a desk, and above the desk were a dozen television screens, all blank. On the wall nearby was a control board. Boff's eyes lit up as they flitted across the array of switches. He ran his hands across them, feeling them, then found a switch marked "On/Off" and turned it to "On".

"Boff!" Charlotte's voice. "What are you doing!"

"It's not ours!" said Jayne. "We shouldn't touch it!"

Boff ignored them. There was a slight humming noise. A few seconds later the television screens sprang into life and displayed a dozen different scenes. Now the others shouted.

"Look! It's the gates of this house!"

Boff looked at the cluster of monitors they were pointing to and realized what they meant. One screen showed the front gates from the inside, another from the outside. Any vehicle standing there could be identified, whether it was waiting to go in or out. Another screen was a close-up near the gates, for recognizing faces, and one was a view of the gates from halfway up the drive where it turned the corner. A fifth showed the drive where it approached the house, two showed the front door in close-up from each side, and several more had scenes they couldn't place.

Boff turned the switch to "Off" again, and all the screens died, along with the humming.

"We'd better leave it as we found it," he said.

They went back along to the kitchen, and Toby was allowed to make them all a cup of tea as penance for his selfish behaviour. He made them some toast as well, and they discussed the situation as they munched and sipped.

"Perhaps he's popped into town," suggested Jayne. "He could be back any minute."

"That doesn't explain the note," said Ben. "It says that he's going to be away for *a few days*."

"All right, then," said Charlotte, "why has he written it to Miss Coates and not to us?"

"Perhaps he's gone mad," said Toby.

"I know!" said Jayne, suddenly animated. "What if it's *us* he's taking away for a few days!"

"I still don't see what Miss Coates has got to do with it," said Boff. "And it wouldn't explain the half-eaten breakfast, either."

"Well—" Jayne stretched her brain to its limits. "—Suppose he just happens to have a cleaner called Miss Coates – she might even be another cousin – and she normally comes in on Saturdays, and he gets a phone call during breakfast and has to rush off, so he scribbles a note for her to feed the cat. But she's ill and doesn't come. Everything gets left as it is, and Mr Blake is delayed and can't leave a message because there's no one here . . ." Her voice trailed off. The faces around her didn't look convinced.

"Mmmm," said Boff. "Some of it might be right."

"It could *all* be right," said Jayne earnestly. "There has to be *some* explanation, doesn't there?"

"Whatever way we look at it," said Ben, "Mr Blake hasn't been here since breakfast. He wouldn't have left his stuff like this if he'd been back."

There was a long pause. Eventually, Boff said slowly, "You realize we'll have to go home if Mr Blake doesn't show up, don't you?"

The others were shocked. Less than an hour ago, they were missing their tree-house back home. But now the thought of leaving Naitagonia before they had had a chance to explore it was more than they could bear.

"Why?"

"Simple," explained Boff. "Because if he doesn't show up soon, we'll have to tell the police."

43

"But why?" said Toby.

"You know what careful plans were made for us to come here," Boff reminded them. "Letters to our parents, and reassurances from Mr Elliott and the SS *Coates*. It's not easy for parents to send their children away with near strangers, especially when we're only ten, eleven and twelve years old – well, I'm *nearly* thirteen. Just think. If they knew we were alone in this huge house in the middle of nowhere with no one to look after us, they'd be furious – after all the promises. And if we have to tell the police what's happened, they'll say 'We'll deal with this' and send us all home again."

Everyone stared at Boff. The silence that followed seemed endless. The trouble with Boff was that he was too realistic most of the time. There was often a danger that his irritating habit of thinking clearly would take the fun out of everything they tried to do. On this occasion, sadly, the other Naitabals realized that he was probably right.

Ben, however, didn't care.

"We could hide," he said, simply.

"What do you mean?" said Charlotte.

"The police wouldn't need to know we were here. We could hide in the woods and try to find Mr Blake ourselves."

Everyone was stunned – and intrigued.

"Our parents wouldn't be worried," Ben went on, "because they'd still be thinking we're here with Mr Blake."

"Yes," said Boff, "but if anything happened to any of us we'd be in deep, deep trouble. They'd never trust us ever again. I'd be in the most trouble because I'm the oldest and supposed to be in charge – not that I mind taking the blame," he added hastily.

"But if we have to tell the police that Mr Blake is missing, they'll want to know who we are," said Jayne.

"Well, we won't tell them, then," said Toby. "They can torture me and pull my fingernails out and break my legs, but they'll never—"

"Yes, thank you, Toby," said Charlotte. "We get the message."

"And I'm still starving hungry," Toby complained, jumping up. "I can't stand it any longer. Toast wasn't enough. I need more food."

"They'll know how to torture you, then, won't they?" said Jayne. "Just stop feeding you for a couple of hours and you'll tell them everything they want to know."

"Or keep waking you up," said Charlotte.

"Come on," said Boff. "We shouldn't waste any more time. We've got to decide what to do. I suggest we make a thorough search of the house and grounds, and if Mr Blake hasn't appeared by eight o'clock, we phone the police."

"And if the cleaner didn't come this morning, the cat hasn't been fed, either," said Jayne. "Poor thing."

"It'll show up if it's hungry," said Toby. "I would."

"We know *you* would."

An hour later, the whole of Blake Island had been thoroughly searched, but no further clue to the mystery was found. Back in the kitchen, they had beans on toast and more drinks and waited for inspiration.

"It's still only seven o'clock," said Jayne at last, when no other ideas were forthcoming. "There's time to find Elliott the cat and feed him."

"Or her," said Charlotte.

"I hardly think Mr Blake would have called it Elliott

if it was a her," said Jayne. "Where's the note?"

Charlotte found it and read it again, even though they more or less knew it word for word. "It is a tom. It says *he* spends most of *his* time in the woods."

The thought of exploring the dark, mysterious woods behind the house was an exciting one, and no one wanted to be left behind to wait for Mr Blake.

"We'll leave a note on the table to say we're looking for Elliott," said Ben. "Then we can all go."

Everyone thought this was a good idea. Charlotte drew a picture of a cat, wrote "NAITABALS" underneath and left it pinned under a marmalade jar.

The hill behind the house was very steep, but no problem for Naitabals who were used to climbing trees and swinging on ropes across rivers. The wood was thick with ancient oaks and beeches. Much of the lower slopes were carpeted with the spent leaves of bluebells. Further up they disappeared, giving way to thicker undergrowth, patches of bramble, and other ankle-ripping tangles.

It was Toby who saw her first.

"Look!" he said, pointing.

The others followed the direction of his arm and saw what looked like an elderly woman in the distance. She was moving along a track a little way above them. They couldn't see her feet. Instead of walking she seemed to be sailing effortlessly, floating like a ghost above the ground.

Hearing them, the woman stopped and turned her head. She had faded yellow hair, a jutty-out chin, and a nose that was short and curved like a ski-jump. She was wrapped up warm in layer upon layer of assorted clothing. As they scrambled up the slope towards her, she started to move again.

"Excuse me," called Charlotte, trying to catch up, "do

you know Mr Blake who lives at Darkwood House?"

But the woman gained speed on the level path as they struggled up the hill. Charlotte called again, but by the time they reached the path, the figure had disappeared, swallowed into the dark woods like a wraith.

"I think she's mad," said Jayne, summing up for all of them. "She must have heard us, because she stopped."

"Frightened of strangers, probably," said Charlotte.

Everyone agreed that the woman was very odd, and after a brief discussion they continued their advance up the hill. They spread out slowly as they went, all calling "puss-puss-puss" or "Elli-Elli-Elliott" as loudly as they could.

Every now and then they turned to look back down the hill, but all they could see was trees. Only occasionally did they get a glimpse of distant scenery, where a tree had fallen, or where an area was mainly filled with younger saplings. They couldn't see anything of Blake Island, Bow Stream or the Bay of Grass.

"Mi-a-ow!"

Jayne stopped.

"Was that one of you?"

"What?"

"That 'mi-a-ow'."

"I didn't mi-a-ow. Did you mi-a-ow, Charlotte?"

"No, I only puss-pussed."

"Did you mi-a-ow, Ben?"

"No. I was Elli-Elli-Elliotting."

"Listen!"

"Mi-aaaa-ow!"

The sound came from further up the wood, and it wasn't far from where Jayne was, in the middle.

"I didn't hear anything!" Boff called from the far side.

"Come this way, then. It's up here."

Jayne climbed several metres further and listened again for the faint sound as the others drew in towards her.

"Stop crashing about, Toby! Listen!"

There was silence, apart from a faint stirring of wind in the treetops and the occasional startled blackbird pinking through the undergrowth.

"Puss-puss-puss-puss-puss," Jayne added encouragingly.

They all heard it then – a pitiful wail.

"Mi-aaaaaaaa-oooooow!"

"It's up a tree!" said Charlotte. "It's stuck, poor thing!"

"Can you see it?"

"No. I think it must be in that oak there."

They all stared into the canopy of the huge oak tree that Charlotte was pointing at. It stood on a little terrace of its own, where the ground had levelled off, and it was covered with ivy. Thick trunks of the creeper climbed up the giant one of the oak, twisting round it like a stick of barley sugar, and showering every space with great bunches of its dark green leaves.

The pitiful cry of the cat came again.

"I wonder how it got up there?" said Ben. There was no doubt now that the sound came from the tree they were admiring. "I suppose it must have run up the ivy."

"Oh, they can run straight up sheer trunks with their sharp little claws," said Jayne. "The only trouble is, they don't know how to get down again."

They had climbed further and had almost reached the base of the tree when Ben, who was in front, cried out.

"LOOK!"

He was pointing straight up the tree on its far side.

"It's a TREE-HOUSE!" squealed Jayne.

"Weeeeeeeeeeeee!" said Toby.

"Mi-aaaaa-oooow!" said the pathetic cat.

"It sounds as if it's inside!" said Charlotte.

"There's a trap-door in the floor," said Ben. "We'll have to get up and get in, somehow."

The discovery of the tree-house was a big enough surprise, but the real shock was yet to come.

Even as they stared up at the trap-door, wondering how they could reach it, it began, very slowly, to open.

CHAPTER SIX

Dinner With the Cat

Five pairs of Naitabal eyes stared as the trap-door opened wide and became a gaping black hole. Moments later, a rope-ladder came curling down towards them, operated by unseen hands. There was no further sound from above, no more pathetic miaowing. The Naitabals stood back, suspicious, throwing worried glances at each other, and wondering who, or what, was inside. Was it a trap?

"Who's there?" Boff called, and Charlotte said, "Puss, puss, puss!" hopefully.

Ben, the ever-adventurous, took hold of the rope-ladder.

Jayne put restraining hands on his shoulders.

"Don't, Ben! It might be a trap!"

"Ben!" said Boff. "Don't!" Then, to the dark hole in the tree-house, "Who's up there?"

Ben shrugged off the warnings.

"Someone's got to find out. If you all hang on to the ladder, whoever it is won't be able to pull it up, will they?"

"No," said Boff, and added in a whisper, "but he can close the trap-door on the rest of us while he's murdering you."

"All right, then," said Ben, relenting slightly, "let's both go up."

50

Boff realized that Ben was determined to carry on, and going up with him seemed to be a good compromise.

Ben stepped on to the first wobbly rung of the ladder. It swung to and fro as his weight took it. Boff stepped on the other side, and they swung in the air face to face as their hands and feet competed for somewhere to hold. They made slow, awkward progress. If it hadn't been such a serious situation, they might have found the idea of two of them climbing a rope-ladder, one on each side, a lot more fun. As it was, all their concentration was on the black void above their heads.

One by one they climbed the rungs, getting better at balancing each other's weight as they went. They stopped a metre from the top, straining to see what was inside, or whom, and ready to drop back to the ground at the slightest hint of danger. They stood there, poised, peering upwards, watching for the slightest threat from within. The others crowded at the bottom, ready to break their fall if they jumped.

"Mi-aaaa-oooow!" came the cry again, definitely from inside the tree-house, and Toby commented, "Don't tell me the cat opened the trap-door!"

A man's voice came from inside.

"No, it wasn't the cat," it said.

It was a voice that they all recognized, and they all shouted at once.

"Mr Blake!"

Mr Blake's face, wrinkled with smiles, appeared suddenly at the entrance. It beamed at the two startled faces of Ben and Boff only a metre away, and it beamed at the more distant, but equally startled ones of Charlotte, Jayne and Toby. Mr Blake looked at his watch with an obvious gesture, and again at the five Naitabals below.

"Mmmm!" he complained, clicking his tongue. "That

took you two and a half hours." There was a friendly frown on his brow, and friendly criticism in his voice. Then he relented a little and added, "Not bad for beginners, I suppose. But I must say I expected a quicker result from the Naitabals!"

"Where's the cat, then?" asked Jayne, looking round.

The five Naitabals were seated in a jagged semi-circle inside the tree-house, still dazed at the turn of events and the rather sudden discovery of Mr Blake, who was now sitting on a bench facing them, beaming like a crescent moon.

"Let me introduce you to Elliott the cat..." he chuckled, then tilted his head and did a loud, pathetic "Mi-aaaa-oooow!"

"That was *brilliant*," said Charlotte, impressed. "We really thought it was a cat stuck up the tree."

"*Isn't* there a cat in here, then?" said Jayne, half disappointed.

"I'm afraid not, my dear."

"You really had us worried," said Boff, "not being at the house to meet us, and leaving that strange note."

"Well, if you remember," said Mr Blake, "the first time we met was in *your* tree-house—"

"The Naitabal hut," corrected Toby.

"... Yes, the Naitabal hut ... So I thought it would be appropriate, when you came to visit me, that we should meet in mine. That's fair, isn't it?"

"You bet!" said Ben.

"I also wanted to see if you were fit for the *other* adventurous tasks I've set for you," Mr Blake went on. "I really thought it would take you about an hour to find me – but it took you two and a half. Now, that's not perfect, but it's not a disastrous start."

"But we really thought you were missing," said Boff. "We didn't know it was a *game*."

"All the best games are like the real thing, aren't they?" said Mr Blake, teasing them. "Didn't you find the first clue helped enough...?" He stared at the slightly blank faces around him. "I mean, you did *know* the whole holiday is a treasure hunt?"

"Yes, we knew it was a treasure hunt..." said Ben.

"There you are, then."

"But we didn't get the first clue."

"What?"

"We didn't know what to think," said Charlotte.

Now it was Mr Blake's turn to look shocked.

"You mean you didn't get my letter?" he said.

"No," said Boff. "Only your invitation."

"No, no. After that. I said I'd write to you before you came, didn't I?"

"Yes," said Ben.

"Well, I did. I addressed it to the Naitabal tree-house."

"When we hadn't heard," Boff said, "we tried telephoning, but we couldn't get an answer."

"But we knew it was all right to come," said Charlotte, "because your invitation said you'd let us know if there was any hitch."

"I see," said Mr Blake. "So you didn't get my letter, addressed to the Naitabal hut, containing the first clue?"

He stared again at the blank faces.

"No, we didn't," said Boff, a little sternly.

"No wonder it took you two and a half hours," said Mr Blake, "if you didn't realize me being missing might be part of the treasure hunt."

"When we got here and couldn't find you," Boff added, "we almost called the police."

Mr Blake threw his head back and laughed.

"Don't worry," he said. "It wouldn't have mattered if you did. I'd already warned them about the clues and told them not to take it too seriously if they got any calls from you."

Boff was alarmed.

"But what if something nasty *had* happened?" he said.

"Well," Mr Blake chuckled. "I'm sure you would have sorted it out."

"When did you start timing us?" said Jayne.

"As soon as the taxi arrived and I had unlocked the gates. That's why I gave the taxi strict instructions *not* to bring you up the drive. It wouldn't have given me enough time to get away, you see. I deliberately left my breakfast things the way you found them so that the house would look like the *Marie Celeste*—"

"I *said* it looked like the *Marie Celeste*!" said Charlotte.

"—And by the time you were walking up to the house, I was well on my way to the tree-house. I was ready to come down at dusk if you couldn't find me."

"The tree-house is great," said Ben. "Almost as good as ours."

Mr Blake raised an eyebrow.

"Almost?"

Charlotte gave Ben a hard poke in the ribs.

"Ben!"

"Oh, er—" began Ben. Then he realized how insulting he'd been, and started to apologize.

Mr Blake interrupted with a laugh.

"I can see you haven't really solved the second clue, either," he said.

"What do you mean?"

"Well, there's no cat."

"Pardon?"

"There's no cat, is there?"

"We know there's no cat *now*," said Ben, "but we still don't understand."

"I do," said Boff, "—well . . . half, anyway. If there isn't a cat – *why did you ask us to feed it*?"

"No, no, no, no, no," said Mr Blake, enjoying himself. Then he quoted from the note he'd left on the kitchen table. " '*Please feed the cat. His name is Elliott, and he spends most of his time in the woods*'!"

Five blank faces stared back at the illuminated one of Mr Blake, but no further clues were forthcoming.

At last Toby's face lit up in triumph.

"*Mr Elliott* built *this* tree-house!" he shouted.

"Yes! At last!"

"He said he was coming to do some building work on your house!" said Ben. "I bet he didn't do anything to your house at all!"

"He meant the *tree*-house!" said Jayne.

"You're dead right!" said Mr Blake. "And now it's yours."

"*What??*"

"The tree-house is yours, I tell you. You don't think I'd expect five Naitabals on a treasure-hunting adventure holiday to slum it in a stuffy old country house with central heating, television, nine bedrooms and five bathrooms, do you? Good gracious, no. Not when there are Naitabal trees everywhere, and a dark Naitabal wood to live in, and Naitabal food everywhere? Not likely! You want to fend for yourselves, don't you? That's what you'd prefer, isn't it?"

"Oh, Mr Blake!" Charlotte and Jayne flung themselves on him, one on each arm. "Yes, please!"

"Thank you!"

"You're wonderful, Mr Blake!"

"Well, let's face it," he said, enjoying this sudden attention, "if it hadn't been for you Naitabals, my business wouldn't have survived. Mrs Blake and I would have been out on the street."

"Mrs Blake? We didn't know there was a Mrs Blake," said Charlotte.

"Oh, yes," said Mr Blake, looking serious for a moment. "There's very much a Mrs Blake. I'll introduce you on Wednesday."

"Where is she?" said Jayne.

"Spending a few days with the little Blakes and the little-little Blakes – the grandchildren. Don't worry, it was all agreed with your parents when I came down to meet them." He smiled again. "No – without you not only would we have lost the house, but the country would have lost an important new invention in the fight against crime – which I shall tell you about later. That's why the tree-house is yours. And the tree-house is just the beginning of my big 'thank you', I promise! Your treasure hunt has only just begun!"

The Naitabals were too excited to speak, and just grinned at each other until Mr Blake spoke again.

"Now – allow me to show you the facilities," he said, getting up. "You'll be completely safe here – *that I can promise.*"

They took it in turns to look through the four small windows, one in each side, which gave out through little tunnels of ivy and oak leaves.

"The woods belong to me, so no one's likely to come through them," Mr Blake explained. "The odd lost hiker, perhaps, or Ruins Annie."

"Ruins Annie?" said Charlotte, turning. "Is that who we saw?"

"We asked if she'd seen you," said Jayne, "but she didn't answer, and we couldn't catch her."

Mr Blake laughed.

"That sounds like Annie!" he said. "Yellow hair and dressed like a jumble sale?"

"Yes," said Charlotte.

"She's a bit eccentric. She lives in a ruined house at the edge of the west woods. That's why she's called Ruins Annie. She owns the place. It burnt down, it wasn't insured, and she didn't have any money to rebuild it. So she lives in the cellar in the winter, and the dining room in the summer – what's left of it." He laughed again. "She might take a fancy to this tree-house, so don't leave it unguarded with the rope-ladder down!

"Now, there's fresh mountain spring water in the stream over yonder," he said, pointing again. "It's been tested and it's safe to drink. And you can light a fire on the flat ground near the tree-house. You know never to light fires when we've had a lot of hot weather and everything's dry, don't you?"

"Yes, Mr Blake."

"But it's OK at the moment – no danger from flying sparks." He paused. "Now, you must come to the house each evening, I think, for a good main meal – that way I'll know you've had something decent, and I won't be accused by your parents of sending you home half starved or malnourished. Shall we say seven o'clock?"

Everyone agreed that seven was perfect, as it would leave them plenty of time after the meal for getting back before dark.

"Now what about this evening? Would you like to come down and have a meal with me?"

"Well . . . we've already had a meal," said Charlotte. "Sort of."

"What d'you mean, 'sort of'?" protested Toby. "That was the best beans on toast you'll ever have. No one does beans on toast better than me. Each separate bean lovingly heated to the perfect temperature . . . Each slice of toast perfectly—"

"Burnt," said Charlotte.

"Even so," said Mr Blake, "it doesn't sound very substantial . . ."

"We had a big packed lunch on the train," said Boff. "I don't know about everyone else, but I'd rather settle in here and get a good night's sleep."

Everyone agreed: now that they were in a new tree-house, they didn't want to leave it.

"Why don't you stay and have something with us, Mr Blake?" Jayne suggested.

"That sounds a nice idea," said Mr Blake. "There's plenty of food in the cupboard here, look."

He opened the cupboard, and they goggled at the huge supply that would keep them going for days.

"And there's an ice-box here with some sausages and bacon and eggs. There's not much room for milk, so you must come down every morning and get a fresh supply from me. And you must get fresh ice-cubes, as well – that's very important."

Suddenly everyone was feeling hungry again and there was a scramble to get down the rope-ladder to light their first real fire. The rope-ladder swung precariously as Mr Blake's substantial weight clung on to it.

"I'll have to show you how to lock the tree-house when you go away," he said, "otherwise you'll have squatters!"

When they were all down, he hauled on a loose rope that entered the tree-house through a hole in the floor.

The rope-ladder magically rolled upwards and disappeared into the trap-door entrance. Then he wound the rope on to a cleat hidden in the ivy and stuffed the trailing end out of sight.

"And now the finishing touch!" he announced.

He led them away from the Naitabal tree for twenty metres, then stooped down near a large patch of bramble. He reached gingerly underneath, drew out a thick bamboo pole, about four metres long, then led them back to the tree-house. He used the pole to push the trap-door closed, and they heard a click. He pushed it again, and it came open.

"It's just a simple device you get on attic trap-doors," he said, clicking it shut again.

"But that means anyone can get in just by pushing it," said Boff, frowning.

Mr Blake looked at Boff closely and grinned and turned the bamboo pole the other way up.

"How about that?" he said.

What Boff and the others hadn't noticed was the window-lock key fixed to its other end. With great skill, Mr Blake guided the cylindrical, toothed key up towards a tiny hole on the edge of the trap-door. When it was in, he gave it a clockwise twist.

"Now try and push it open!" he said.

They couldn't, of course. They spent the next ten minutes practising the locking and unlocking procedure, and opening and closing the trap-door.

"When you retire for the night you take the pole in with you," said Mr Blake, "—yes, it does fit. And when you go away, make sure you hide the pole in the brambles."

Now everyone was even hungrier.

"Come on!" squealed Charlotte. "Sausages and toast cooked over an open fire!"

CHAPTER SEVEN

Eception-rong Arty-pong

It was nearly eleven o'clock. Six bodies glowed orange, spread around the open fire that flickered and danced in their midst. It was pitch black in the woods behind them. Everyone was deliriously happy.

"Best meal I've ever had!" groaned Mr Blake. He was lying flat on the ground, holding his stomach. The Naitabals were scattered all around in various postures of painful over-exposure to hot sausages.

"My stomach hurts!" said Toby.

"Mine, too!"

"And mine."

Charlotte's tortured voice joined in.

"Does anyone want the last sausage?"

The night air was filled with unanimous, painful cries.

"No!"

"When do we get our next clue, Mr Blake?" asked Ben, full, and hurting, but happy.

"Oh, yes, I'd forgotten about that. It's around here, of course. Each clue leads you to the next. You'll have to find it."

"Not now," groaned Jayne.

"You'll need the first one as well," Mr Blake said. "You can't solve the final problem without the first clue."

"But we've done the first part, surely?" said Boff.

Mr Blake rolled his head from side to side on the grassy ground.

"All I can say," he said, "is that you still need the first clue. But don't worry. I've got a copy of it in my briefcase down at the house. I'll write it out again and give it to you in the morning when you come to get the milk. It's a pity you didn't get it in the post, isn't it?"

Soon Jayne sat up and threw a few more dry sticks on to the fire.

"It's lovely and dark!" she said suddenly, peering into the blackness. "Let's teach Mr Blake Naitabal Morse!"

In spite of their bloated stomachs, everyone thought this was a great idea, including Mr Blake. He wasn't looking forward to going back to his house and leaving the Naitabals to have all the fun.

"I'll have to go back soon," he said, "but I'd love to learn Naitabal Morse first."

"It's much easier than ordinary Morse," said Charlotte. "It was Boff's idea. It's so easy that we all learnt it on the train."

"It'll probably take me a month, then," said Mr Blake.

Briefly, Charlotte explained the code, using a Naitabal torch.

"So all you've got to remember, if you're using a Naitabal torch," she finished, "is dot, dash, red, green, wiggle."

"Dot, dash, red, green, wiggle," chanted Mr Blake. "No problem."

They were all too full to be bothered to spread out much into the woods, so they stayed round the fire, telling each other (slow) jokes in Naitabal Morse. They were all impressed at how quickly Mr Blake picked it up.

They were so busy concentrating, laughing and joking that no one noticed a car's headlights flashing briefly like lightning on the drive below the trees. Certainly no one heard the quiet hum of its engine.

"You must never tell anyone else about Naitabal Morse," said Charlotte, when they had all had enough.

Then Boff said something that had been on his mind for some time.

"Why do you have all those security cameras at the entrance, Mr Blake?"

"Simple," he said. "That's the business I'm in. Security. It makes a nice display if I have clients visiting, but it also keeps the industrial spies at bay."

"Industrial spies?" asked Jayne. "What are they?"

"Spies who work hard," said Toby.

"Don't be silly, Toby," said Charlotte. "That's *industrious* spies."

"Industrial spies are people in companies who spy on other companies' products. It might be anything from a company trying to pinch the recipe for someone else's cakes, or an aircraft manufacturer stealing another manufacturer's engine design. In my case, I've invented a revolution in security. It will put most burglars out of business, I can assure you. That's why I needed money so badly when we met earlier this year. I was running out of it, and I couldn't persuade the banks to lend me any more. I didn't have enough to finish the project. Then you found it for me. Without you, I would have lost everything. As it is, it can all go ahead. Thanks to you Naitabals."

"What have you invented, then?" said Boff, interested.

"Ah! That would be telling! I'm presenting my idea to the National Police Conference in Cardiff in a few days' time, and I hope to be lodging patent applications at the same time. Until then, it's safest if I don't tell anyone."

"It sounds exciting," said Boff.

"I'm still giving it its final field-testing, you see. I want to make sure it's flawless before I unleash it on the public and the patents office. It is exciting, yes. And that reminds me . . ." Suddenly, Mr Blake's face went pale in the flickering firelight. He held a steadying hand to his stomach and raised himself to his feet.

"What's the matter, Mr Blake?" said Jayne. "Are you ill?"

"No, it's nothing. I've just remembered – I didn't lock the gates after you came in – and the house isn't locked either, of course. There's me talking about security and gates and barbed wire and cameras. It's not much use if I forget to lock it, is it? Anyway, there are a few things I must prepare for tomorrow, so I'd better get going. I'll leave you to find everything else for yourselves, if that's all right. If there's any problem, or if you get hungry for anything, come straight down – or if there's an emergency, just press the little red button in the tree-house – that'll ring in the main house and bring me running – well, puffing and panting, anyway."

The other Naitabals gingerly eased themselves into sitting positions.

"You lock yourselves in, now," warned Mr Blake. "These woods are as safe as anywhere, but I don't want to take any risks with you Naitabals."

"We'll lock up straight away, don't worry."

Jayne lent her Naitabal torch to Mr Blake. He switched it to white and started making his way down the hill in the darkness. They watched the thin pale beam until it was swallowed up by the trees.

The Naitabals were ready for sleep by this time.

"We'll have to clear everything up," said Charlotte. "Otherwise any passing tramps will know we're here."

They tidied up, dowsed the fire, and climbed the rope-ladder with great difficulty, still aching from surfeits of sausages. When they had hauled in the ladder and the bamboo pole and secured the trap-door, Ben was the first to discover another problem.

"Oh, no!" he said. "There are sleeping-bags here, but all our luggage is still in the house! We'll have to go and get it."

"No, we won't," Charlotte reminded him. "Naitabals sometimes go to sleep with their clothes on."

"Oh, yes," said Ben, grinning. "So they do."

Not many minutes later, they were asleep.

Mr Blake made his way carefully down the steep slopes, which grew more treacherous where the ground was thick with bluebell leaves. He slipped on to his bottom once or twice, but he was used to that. He had spent much of the last few weeks carrying planks of wood up the same slopes, supplying Mr Elliott with enough to build the Naitabals' new tree-house. The only difference now was that it was dark, his stomach was still painfully heavy with hot sausages, and he was handicapped by having to hold the torch.

He felt that everything had gone perfectly. The children were obviously delighted with their new tree-house. The looks on their faces were reward enough without all the hundreds of times they must have thanked him.

He clambered down the final slope and dropped on to the path that ran high up along the back of the house at roof level. The house below looked dark and forbidding, huddled in the shadows. He switched off his torch for a moment and stood in the blackness, savouring the starless sky and the near-silence. Only the faintest whisper of a breeze ruffled the treetops around him. Across the bed of the valley, perhaps two miles away, a few tiny farm-house lights pricked the black hills like pin-holes in a sheet of black paper.

He shivered and walked on. At the end of the path he reached into a clump of overgrown bushes and closed his fingers around a familiar handle. He sighed with relief as he pulled the black briefcase from its hiding place.

He made his way down the steps of the overgrown kitchen garden, whistling to keep unthinkable beasts at bay, then along to the porch at the side of the house.

The door to the outside toilet was ajar, and he decided to pay a visit. He went in and put the briefcase on the floor. He smiled at how he'd left out the breakfast things to make the children think they'd found the *Marie Celeste*. He smiled even more at how well it had all worked. The looks on their faces when he had opened the trap-door of the tree-house! That moment was worth all the successful businesses in the world! He hoped there were more to come.

He flushed the toilet and emerged, opened the side door of the house and went in. He stepped into the old flagstoned kitchen, switched on the light, and blinked, unaccustomed to the brightness.

Two men were sitting there.

Five minutes later, the house was in darkness and a midnight-blue estate car was coasting down the drive. There were three men inside, and one of them was wondering if the Naitabals would find the briefcase he had left in the outside loo, or understand the scribbled note on the kitchen table.

66

CHAPTER EIGHT

He Especially Likes Prawns

It was Toby who woke up first.

If any of the Naitabals had placed bets on who would be first to wake up the following morning, none of them would have bet on Toby. Not even Toby would have bet on Toby. He slept twice as much as the others, and it usually took a ninety-decibel thunderclap or a small earthquake to rouse him from his slumber.

But Toby woke up first. It might have been the excitement of going to sleep in a new tree-house in an unexplored wood. Or it might have been the fact that he'd spent half the previous day sleeping in the luggage rack of the train compartment.

Whatever caused it, Toby woke up first.

He stared at his watch and found it difficult to believe that it said only half-past six. He couldn't remember ever seeing it say half-past six before – not in the morning, anyway. At first he thought he had overslept and that it was half-past six the next evening. But he noticed that the other four Naitabals were still in their sleeping-bags, and still fast asleep. He shook his watch. The digital seconds were still counting. Jayne's leg was sticking out of the side of her sleeping-bag where the zip had come open. To make sure he wasn't dreaming, Toby pinched it. The leg twitched and Jayne grunted.

He obviously wasn't dreaming.

He sat up and stared at the unfamiliar sight of four Naitabals fast asleep. Usually, he woke up to the sight of four Naitabals fully dressed and fast awake. True, they were fully dressed inside the sleeping-bags, but there was no sign of movement coming from any of them – apart from Jayne, who suddenly seemed a bit restless.

He stood up, carefully stepped out of his sleeping-bag and looked around. Dim light was filtering through the leaves that waved across the four small windows. It shone most strongly from the east, where the sun was struggling through the treetops that spread as far as he could see in the distance.

He put his jumper on (the only thing he'd taken off, apart from trainers and socks) but didn't bother with footwear. Going barefoot was much better. Then he remembered the nasty brambles. He compromised by putting on just the trainers, without socks. He quietly unbolted the trap-door and rolled out the rope-ladder. The draught got to Jayne's exposed leg, and she was doing up the zip in her sleep as Toby carefully lowered himself to the ground.

The tree-house, unless you knew it was there, was almost impossible to see. If you were coming towards it up the hill, it was invisible. It was possible to spot it if you were coming down the hill, but difficult. He decided they would have to make sure by adding more camouflage on the upper side.

His next discovery was so exciting that it sent him hurrying back to see if any of the others were awake.

He was pleased to see Jayne standing at the bottom of the ladder, yawning and having a good stretch.

"Toby! I don't believe it! You're up!"

"Are any of the others awake?" said Toby, ignoring the insult.

"No. I had a nasty dream. I dreamt my leg was caught in one of those horrible animal traps, and I woke up. How about you?"

"I just found myself awake. I've been up for half an hour. Come and see what I've found."

Jayne followed him down through the trees until the Naitabal hut was just out of sight, then stopped. She goggled at the notice on the tree ahead of them. It was drawing-pinned to the bark, and it said "DEATH SLIDE" in big letters. Below them, beyond it, the ground dropped away vertically into a deep hollow. A thick piece of rope was stretched from a branch high above their heads. It went across the hollow and diagonally down the hill where it ended on the high branch of a distant tree. On the rope, attached to a metal pulley, were two leather straps.

"We can ride down the hill on it!" said Toby.

Jayne clapped her hands together.

"Come on," she said, "let's try it! You go first. You found it."

Toby unwound a thin piece of rope that was coiled round a branch. It was attached to the pulley, and could be used to haul it back to the top of the long rope.

"Look! When I've gone down, you can pull it back up with the rope."

Toby had to jump slightly to grab the straps while Jayne held on to the small rope. As soon as Toby was safely hanging, she let go. With a scream of exhilaration, Toby went hurtling down the big rope. It sagged even further as he went, but the sag was just enough to slow him to a halt as he reached the far tree.

"Wow! It's brilliant!" he shouted back. His voice echoed across Naitagonia.

Jayne wasted no time in hauling the pulley back. She discovered that just hanging the rope over the branch was sufficient to hold the slide ready for action. When it was steady she leapt in the air and grabbed the straps.

She screamed the air out of her lungs as she rocketed downwards with the metal wheel whirring and buzzing above her head. For a few horrible seconds she thought she would smash into the branch at the bottom and go flying off into a patch of brambles. But the sag in the rope slowed her down in time. Toby was waiting, grinning all over his face, as she came to a stop.

"Brilliant!" she said.

Then she saw what else Toby had seen. There was another death slide leading from the same branch where the first one finished. And after that, in the distance, was a third one that would take them almost to the back of Blake Island.

They had two more runs each, then left them primed for action as they made their way breathlessly up to the Naitabal hut to tell the others.

"All we need now is a ski lift!" said Jayne, panting.

The others had heard the shouts and screams, got up, and were already starting down the wood towards the noise. When they were shown the slides, all thoughts of breakfast promptly evaporated, and they spent the next hour and a half playing on them.

By then they were all hungry. They decided that preparation of meals would be supervised in alphabetical order, so Ben and Boff were first to get breakfast.

After breakfast there were so many things to do, the Naitabals didn't know where to begin.

"I think we should find the next clue," said Charlotte.

"Mr Blake said it wasn't far from here and we'd find it easily."

"I think we should explore first," said Ben. "We've got to make a map of Naitagonia."

"I vote we have more goes on the Death Slides," said Toby.

"I think we should go and see Mr Blake," said Jayne, "and say good morning. It's half-past nine."

"All right," said Boff. "We can get some fresh milk and some more ice to put in the ice-box."

"And get our luggage," said Jayne.

It was agreed that a visit to Mr Blake was next.

"We can get down using the Death Slides," said Toby. "It'll take about six times as long to get us *all* down, but it'll be worth it."

Half an hour later, five Naitabals stood at the front door of Mr Blake's house and rang the bell. There was no answer, and Charlotte said jokingly, "Perhaps he's like Toby and doesn't get up until the afternoon."

"Huh!" said Toby, "I was up at half-past six this morning, which is more than I can say for you."

Charlotte looked into the sky to see if any pigs were flying past, while Ben rang the bell again.

There was still no answer, and Boff tried the door. It opened.

"Mr Blake!" he called. "Can we come in?"

By the time Boff had repeated it, they were all inside anyway. They went to the bottom of the wide staircase and called again.

There was still no answer, and Toby and Jayne wandered along to the kitchen.

"Oh dear," said Jayne. "We forgot to clear up our tea

71

and toast things from yesterday. And Mr Blake still hasn't cleared up his breakfast things from yesterday – and there's more cups. Come on, let's wash them up, Toby."

It was then they saw the note. It wasn't the same piece of paper that they'd found the day before. This one as written on the back of a torn-off piece of a cornflakes packet. The words were hastily scribbled, but they were almost the same. The note said:

"*Dear Miss Coates, I've had to slip away for a day or two. Please find Elliott the cat and feed him. He especially like prawns. Charles Blake.*"

"What's he playing at this time?" said Boff. "The note's exactly the same, except he's talking about Elliott liking prawns."

"And Elliott the cat doesn't exist, so how can he like prawns anyway?" said Ben.

"It's the second clue," said Charlotte. "Mr Blake said we'd find it without too much trouble."

Just like the day before, they searched the house. Again, there was no sign of their host. None of the beds looked as if they had been slept in, but of course they might have been straightened up afterwards. Even so, there was no other evidence to show that he had been there at all – except for the new note and the extra crockery that Toby and Jayne were clearing up.

"He had *four* cups of coffee," said Jayne. "In *four* different cups."

"He said he had things to do before tomorrow," said Boff.

"He must be hiding somewhere *else* in the woods," said Charlotte.

"Another tree-house," said Ben.

"Or the ruins," said Jayne. "I bet it's the ruins."

"Not very likely," said Boff. "It's too simple."

"I bet the answer's in the packet of prawns," said Jayne. "Let's look for it."

They spent the next ten minutes searching the kitchen and the deep-freeze for cat food in general, and prawns in particular.

"Nothing," said Ben. "No prawns anywhere."

"That reminds me," said Charlotte. "I must take fresh ice-cubes for the ice-box."

Boff's face was set as his brain worked on the new problem. "It seems a bit odd that Mr Blake should give us the same clue again. There's something wrong with the whole thing."

"Why?" said Jayne. "It's meant to be a puzzle. That's why he's done it. And the clue isn't *quite* the same. It's got the bit about the prawns."

"But he said we'd find the second clue near the tree-house, not the *house*."

"He was just teasing us. He knew we'd come down for milk. He said we should. He knew we'd find the note, just like yesterday."

Boff still wasn't satisfied. He thought for another few minutes while the others checked again for anything to do with prawns.

"I know!" said Ben. "I bet there are prawns in our larder in the tree-house! And the next *real* clue is inside it! That explains why he said the next clue was near the tree-house!"

There was general agreement that this sounded sensible, but Boff still wasn't a hundred per cent happy.

"I'll stay here and see what else I can find," he said.

"Well, I'll stay with Boff," said Jayne. "You three go and look in the tree-house."

"And take your luggage as well," said Boff.

They fetched all the bags from where they had left

them in the hall. Jayne and Boff brought theirs into the kitchen so they wouldn't forget them, then Ben, Charlotte and Toby set off. Jayne followed Boff into the room where all the security equipment was housed.

"The television room," said Jayne.

They were half surprised to find that the system was now switched on. They could see the view of the drive, the views of the front door, and the views of the gates, still closed.

"I wonder if they're locked," said Boff.

"Yes," said Jayne. "And I wonder how Mr Blake gets in and out when he's leaving the house?"

"Probably has an infra-red remote controller, like you use for your television at home. He just presses a button to open the gates as he approaches."

Amongst the long line of switches, Boff found the one labelled "Lock/Unlock".

"It's set to 'Lock'," he said, pointing. "It was set to 'Unlock' when we came yesterday. So if Mr Blake has gone away, he must have the control with him."

"But his car's still here," said Jayne. "I saw it in the yard as we came down."

"Are you sure it's his?"

"Positive. It was here yesterday and it's the same one he had when he visited Miss Coates."

"Perhaps he's got two."

"There weren't two here yesterday when he was hiding in the tree-house."

Boff seemed relieved.

"That means he's still here somewhere, then."

They collected their luggage and set off back towards the tree-house.

"It doesn't matter about leaving the front door unlocked," said Boff. "Mr Blake doesn't seem to worry.

Anyway, the gates on the drive are locked, so no one can get in without an infra-red control."

It was tiring climbing the hill with their luggage, and they paused several times to rest. As they neared the Naitabal hut they were greeted by Toby, who had seen them and was coming down to give them a hand.

"No prawns," he announced.

"Never mind," said Jayne. "Elliott the cat will have to starve."

"But we've found another clue instead!"

"Where?"

"In the ice-box – when we were putting fresh ice-cubes in and looking for prawns."

They dropped their luggage and sprinted. They found Ben and Charlotte sitting on the ground, studying a tiny wet rag of waterproof paper. Charlotte held it up triumphantly.

"It was frozen inside one of the ice-cubes," she said, offering it to Boff. "We took turns sucking it to get the message out."

Boff withdrew his outstretched hand. He decided suddenly that he didn't want to read it himself, after all.

"What does it say?" he said.

Charlotte took it back and read:

> *"Where the Virginia creeper climbs,*
> *Above the cloud the silver lines,*
> *Travel where the compass points,*
> *See the stone the stream anoints."*

CHAPTER NINE

Fat-Bang-Face

Over drinks of lemonade the Naitabals studied the clues they had found so far.

"The one we found on the kitchen table – let's call it the Prawn Clue," said Charlotte, " – must be a copy of the first clue Mr Blake sent, but we didn't get. *Mr Blake said he'd give us a copy, didn't he?* Don't you see?"

"But it doesn't make *sense* as a first clue," said Boff, who was more worried than the others about the strange sequence of events. "If it was the first clue – which we know we've already solved – where did the prawns come in?"

"In the ice-box, of course," said Toby.

"But there weren't any prawns there," Boff protested.

"Mr Blake said we'd still need it," said Ben. "And if it is the first clue, we don't need it, do we?" Then he added vaguely, "Perhaps there are two parts to each clue . . ."

Boff took a clean piece of paper and summarized what they knew of the clues so far. He wrote:

Clue 1 – Unknown, sent to the Naitabal hut at home.
Clue 2 – On arrival, referred to Elliott in the woods –
        Solved as meaning the tree-house that he built.
Clue 3 – Clue 1?? Reference to cat Elliott and prawns.

Boff frowned hard at them, hoping that something would make sense, but nothing did.

"We'll have to search the wood again," said Ben. "It's bound to mean we've got to listen for Mr Blake miaowing somewhere else."

"Or making a noise like a prawn," suggested Toby. "Does anyone know what sort of noise prawns make?"

"Car prawns go *paaarp*," said Ben.

"What about a fog prawn," said Toby. "You can hear those right across the English Channel."

"Mr Blake must be thinking how stupid we are by now," said Jayne, ignoring them. "He's given us practically the same clue, and we haven't even *started* looking for him yet. It's ages since we found the note."

This made everyone feel guilty, so they spread out from the bottom of Naitagonia and worked their way to the top. It was all much as they had done the day before, but this time they were spaced much further apart.

"Give a double Naitabal whistle if you find anything," Ben suggested before they started climbing.

Half an hour later they had all reached the summit of Naitagonia. The woods ended with a three-strand barbed-wire fence that cut it off from huge green pastures full of sheep, high up on the hilltop and overlooking the countryside for miles around. They climbed the fence, walked to the far side of the first field, and gazed down on the town that lay huddled in the valley below, bathed in a faint blue haze.

"Civilization," murmured Ben.

Their curiosity satisfied, they spread out again and went

77

back down through Naitagonia, calling for Elliott the cat, but hearing no answering miaows.

Boff decided to go to the Naitabal hut and study the clues again while the others carried on exploring. He took yet another piece of paper and wrote the words "HE ESPECIALLY LIKES PRAWNS" on it in big letters. Why would Mr Blake write "He especially likes prawns" when there wasn't really a cat and there weren't any prawns either? He couldn't believe the ice-box answer. If that had been the answer, the clue would have been taped to a packet of prawns, not buried in an ice-cube. Mr Blake had hinted at the importance of changing the ice-cubes. They should have listened more carefully to everything Mr Blake had said.

Boff furrowed his brow again in concentration as the sounds of the other Naitabals' voices faded into the hillside. Ten minutes later, he was hurtling down to the house to use the telephone.

"Hello, Mum? Yes, it's me. We're fine, thanks. I was wondering if you'd had a letter for us? It was addressed to the Naitabal tree-house, but the postman wouldn't have been able to deliver it. I just thought he might have put it through our door. No? If it does turn up, will you post it to us? Thanks, Mum. What? Oh, yes, lovely and comfortable, thanks. The best beds we've ever slept in. I will. Thanks. Bye."

His fingers busied on the buttons again.

"Hello – Mrs Maddison? It's Barry Offord here. Yes, Charlotte's fine, thanks. We're all fine. I was just ringing to ask if you've had a letter delivered to your house, addressed to us in the Naitabal tree-house? No? Oh, well, never mind. If it does arrive, could you send it to Mr Blake's? Thanks. And could you give me Cedric Morgan's number? Thanks . . . Got it. Thanks . . . Bye."

Boff took a deep breath and started tapping the number.

The last thing he wanted to do was to ask Cedric a favour. Favours to Cedric meant favours in return, and to Cedric that could mean only one thing – a loan of the Naitabal tree-house. For that reason, it was always securely locked in the Naitabals' absence. Cedric was fairly brainless, but he possessed plenty of animal cunning.

Boff's finger finished tapping and he heard the ringing tone.

Cedric Morgan came running in to the telephone and was more than surprised to find Boff on the other end of it. He didn't know quite what to think at first. Contact between the Naitabals and Cedric's gang was usually confined to the hurling of insults or challenges (from a safe distance by the Igmopong) whenever they happened to meet. As Cedric's garden was sandwiched between Charlotte's and Mr Elliott's, this was a daily occurrence. Telephone calls, however, were unheard of. With a sinking feeling, he wondered if it was anything to do with the letter.

"Hello, Cedric speaking."

"It's Boff. Barry Offord. From two doors down."

"I know where you live, stupid," said Cedric, feeling that attack was the best method of defence. "What do you want?" Then his voice went smooth and oily. "By the way, Boff, I'm glad you phoned. We're having a lovely time in your tree-house. We got in through the roof. We didn't damage it *very* much, and Andy says he can fix it – if we can find enough decent wood. And my sister Doris dropped a tin of red paint inside. It wouldn't come off, so we spread it around a bit and there was enough to paint all the walls and the floor as well. I hope you like it when you see it. It should be dry by then."

Boff ignored the fairy-tale. He could always tell when Cedric was making things up because his voice changed into a higher sneer.

"I hope you didn't let my tarantula escape," he retorted.

There was a short silence from Cedric.

"No. We fed it and put it back in its box."

"That's funny, Cedric. We haven't got a tarantula."

There was another short silence.

"I was just teasing," said Cedric. "We didn't see one, really."

"You might be able to help me, though."

Cedric knew then it was about the letter he had stolen. He immediately put up his guard.

"I don't know if I *want* to help you."

"Someone sent a letter. It was addressed to us at the Naitabal hut, so I wondered if it's been left near the tree anywhere? Pinned to it, perhaps?"

There was a third short silence.

"Yes – yes, I believe I can see an envelope pinned to the tree from here."

Boff winced at the pathetic lie. He knew that Cedric's telephone was fixed in the front hall. It was impossible to see the Naitabal oak from there.

"Could you get it?" he said.

Cedric, greatly relieved, had at last found a way to cover up his crime – and get a reward as well.

"Depends."

"Depends on what?"

"Depends what it's worth."

"It's not very important," said Boff. "We just wanted to know if it arrived, that's all."

"Don't you want to see in it?"

"I wouldn't mind, if it's no trouble."

"You mean, you want me to open it?"

"Yes, please."

"I'll get it. Hold on a minute."

Cedric dropped the receiver and rushed in a panic into his garden. He vaguely remembered screwing the envelope up and throwing it away somewhere near the tree-house. He looked round and soon saw it, a scruffy brown paper ball. He grabbed it, opening it out and smoothing it as he went back to the house. He picked up the telephone again.

"I've got it," he said.

"Good," said Boff. "What does it say?"

"What's it worth?"

"Well – " Boff hesitated. The only reason he'd rung was to find out if the first clue matched any of the ones they'd already found. Only then could he try to unscramble the others. At the same time, he knew that Cedric would want free access to the Naitabal tree-house. He wasn't sure if it was worth that much – especially when Mr Blake had told them that he would write out a copy of the first clue.

"What's the first word in the letter?" he said at last.

"I'm not telling you that. Not until you tell me what it's worth."

"I'll give you a pound."

"A pound? Pooh! I can get a pound off my dotty Aunt Liz any time. She forgets. I ask her for a pound and she gives me one, and ten minutes later I can just ask her for another. Then she forgets she's given me one and she gives me another. I can keep on doing that all day until her money runs out – if my mother isn't listening."

"All right, then," said Boff, "two pounds. Final offer."

"Pooh, no! I'll read you the letter and then you'll not give me the two pounds. I know what you're like."

This told Boff more about Cedric than it told about himself. Not keeping a promise was just the sort of thing Cedric would do – and frequently did.

"What do you want, then?'

"You know what I want. Your tree-house until you get back."

"Oh yes? And when we get back, you won't get out of it? Like you did last time?'

"We would get out. Promise."

Boff tried another tactic.

"Oh, it doesn't matter," he said. "I don't need to know what's in the letter that badly. I'll find out another way."

Cedric realized in a panic that he was about to finish up with nothing. True, he could throw the incriminating envelope away now, but even two pounds was better than nothing. He decided to bargain.

"No, wait – look." A note of desperation crept into his voice. "We'll have your tree-house for one day, OK? Mr Elliott can let us in in the morning and then lock it up again in the evening. You just phone and tell him that it's OK. OK?"

Boff was tempted. He had the other clues spread out by the telephone and he really needed to know if the one about prawns was the copy of the first clue that Mr Blake had promised. He didn't want Cedric messing about in their tree-house back home, but . . .

"OK," he said. "If you read me the message, I'll telephone Mr Elliott and tell him to let you in for a whole day this week."

"*Yes!*" Cedric gripped the telephone receiver under his

chin and used both hands to open the flap of the brown envelope. He pulled out the single crumpled sheet inside. As he looked at it, his eyes bulged and he felt his face getting hotter and hotter. He checked inside the envelope again. It was the only sheet inside. He turned it over. It was blank on the back.

"Well?" said Boff's anxious voice. "What does it say?"

Cedric couldn't tell him that the original sheet was missing. He couldn't tell Boff that the new one was in Charlotte's seven-year-old brother Harry's writing, and that it said:

HELLO FAT-BANG-FACE

"What does it say?" Boff asked again.

"I can't read it," said Cedric. "The lights have just fused."

"Take it to the window, read it, and come back."

"I – I can't. It's gone dark outside as well. It must be a total eclipse. Yes! Someone said there was going to be a total eclipse today."

Boff's patience was running thin.

"Get a torch, then. I'll wait."

"My – my batteries have run out, and—"

"Cedric! There's no power cut, there's no total eclipse, and your torch has almost certainly got batteries. Do you want a day in our tree-house, or don't you?"

"Yes, of course I do. I – I – Can I ring you back in five minutes? Just five minutes?"

"OK."

Boff sighed and gave Cedric the number.

Boff was so shocked at Cedric's sudden retreat that he

stared at the telephone receiver as if it had somehow sent the wrong message. It was unbelievable that Cedric should turn down a chance to stay in the Naitabal hut for a day, and it was equally unbelievable that Mr Blake's letter said nothing. He wondered what was going on.

Five minutes later the telephone rang and Cedric was on the other end.

"Well?" said Boff.

"I don't understand it, really," said Cedric, sounding like an oil slick. "That's why I didn't read it out. I wanted to make sure I was reading it properly, so I've rehearsed it, and—"

"Get on with it," snapped Boff, irritated.

"It says,

> *Hire a taxi and get inside,*
> *And when you're in, go for a ride.*
> *Mr Elliott's like a cat,*
> *Climbing trees in his bowler hat.*' "

Cedric was proud of it. It was the quickest poem he had ever written. It was very close to what he remembered of the original, as close as made no difference.

"There!" he said proudly. "Will you phone Mr Elliott now and tell him to let us into your tree-house?"

Cedric didn't like the horrible silence that followed. He suspected that Boff would go back on his word now that he had read him the message – well, virtually the same message. He was just about to voice this suspicion when Boff's voice crackled on the line.

"Why aren't you reading me the real one?" it said.

"W-what? That was the real one."

"No, it wasn't. That was something you made up. What have you done with it?"

"Honestly, Boff, I—"

But almost at the same moment as Boff started puzzling over Cedric's odd behaviour, he noticed something curious about the prawns message.

"Well, frogs in my pond . . .!" he began, while Cedric spluttered more excuses a hundred and ninety miles away. "Listen, Cedric," he interrupted. "Will you read me the real one, or what?"

"I've just *read* it, I—"

"Well, if you change your mind, post it to us – Mrs Maddison's got the address."

Boff slammed the phone down. He rushed from Blake Island and back to the Naitabal hut. The others were there, dumping huge armfuls of firewood on to a growing heap. Charlotte was waving a map of Naitagonia.

"Boff! We wondered where you'd got to!"

Boff cast the comment aside. His face was even more serious than usual, almost grim.

"I've just worked out the prawns message," he said through his teeth.

"Well? What is it?"

"What does it mean?"

"It's so simple, I don't know why I didn't see it before," Boff complained. "If you take the first letters of 'He Especially Likes Prawns', it spells HELP."

CHAPTER TEN

Oranges and Apples

"It's just a coincidence," said Jayne.

"I don't think so," said Boff.

"Just another clue," said Toby. "That's all. Perhaps the first letters of the other clues spell things."

Boff held them for all to see and shook his head.

"No, they don't. I've checked."

"What do you think's happened, then?" said Ben.

"Mr Blake's disappeared, that's what's happened," said Charlotte.

Boff nodded gravely.

"Look at the second note again," he said. " 'Please find Elliott the cat and feed him. He especially likes prawns.' Well, who *is* Elliott the cat?" he prompted.

"Mr Blake, of course," said Jayne. "It was Mr Blake we found miaowing in the tree-house, so 'Elliott the cat' must mean Mr Blake."

"Exactly," said Boff. "So now read the note again, putting Mr Blake where it says Elliott the cat: it reads 'Please find *Mr Blake* and feed him. *HELP.*' It's a note written to *us*, that's what it is."

"We know it's a note to us," said Jayne. "That's what he did before. It was just a clue to lead us to the tree-house. This is a clue to lead us to something else."

Boff shook his head again.

"This clue's too similar to the first one. That's what worried me all along. And he wouldn't say 'HELP' if he didn't mean it."

"I bet he's been *kidnapped*," said Ben.

Boff considered.

"I don't know about kidnapped, but he's in trouble of some kind – and we've already wasted a lot of time."

"What sort of trouble?" said Jayne.

"I've no idea," said Boff. "But I think we ought to tell the police, don't you?"

The others exchanged glances.

"Telling the police might mean being sent home," said Charlotte. "You said it. I think we should try to find Mr Blake ourselves first . . ."

The grim look that lingered on Boff's face was enough of an answer for Charlotte, but he still put it into words.

"He might be in danger – *real* danger, I mean, not fairy-tale stuff."

"Come on, then," said Ben. "We'd better go down and do it now. We've wasted loads of time already."

They locked the Naitabal hut with the key on the pole, hid the pole, and set off.

Inside Mr Blake's house they huddled round the telephone as Boff dialled nine-nine-nine.

"Hello, which service do you require?" – a woman's voice.

"Police."

There was a momentary pause, then a man's voice came on the line, sounding very official.

"Police. Can I help?"

"Hello, my name is Barry Offord, and I'm speaking from Darkwood House . . ."

"Ah, yes . . ." the policeman's voice suddenly changed to a friendly, unhurried sort of tone.

"Well, we think that Mr Blake has been kidnapped—"

To Boff's surprise, there was the sound of raucous laughter at the other end.

"Don't worry about that, son," said the voice, unable to control itself. "Mr Blake warned us that you might phone and say he was missing."

Boff suddenly remembered Mr Blake's words after his first disappearance: *"Don't worry. I warned the police about the clues, and told them not to take any phone calls seriously."*

"But you don't understand," Boff said. "*He really is missing.* He's written us a note and it really means help, and—"

The laughter crackled in his ear again, and he heard what sounded like a knee being slapped. "He's a great joker is that Charlie Blake! *Exactly* what he told me would happen!" The voice tried to go official again, without much success. "Don't you worry about it, son. He'll turn up! It's just a game! He told me to tell you – *whatever happens, it's all part of the game!*"

"Even if we find him lying in a pool of blood?" Boff retorted. He was irritated by the policeman now, and sarcasm was the only weapon he had left.

To the sound of more merriment, the policeman agreed that if they *did* find Mr Blake in a pool of blood, that was different and they could call him straight away. Then he guffawed again and rang off.

Boff turned to the others and repeated the gist of the conversation.

"He didn't believe me," he said. "Mr Blake told him not to worry if we telephoned about him disappearing – that it was all a game. Unfortunately, it's just backfired. Now it really *has* happened, they don't believe us."

"That's what happened when the shepherd boy cried

'Wolf!'," said Charlotte. "There was no wolf the first few times he called, and when a wolf really came, everyone ignored him."

"And he got eaten," added Toby cheerfully, feeling that Charlotte had missed out the best bit of the story.

"Phone him again," said Jayne. "*Make* him listen!"

"Yes. Tell him we've just found Mr Blake lying in a pool of blood."

"Don't say things like that, Toby!" said Jayne. "Even as a joke."

"Boff started it."

Just then they heard a bleep, and all heads turned.

"It came from the television room!" said Ben. He was first to get there, and the others piled in behind.

On the display panel, a red light was flashing. On the screen nearest the door they could see a car drawn up at the gates, and the gates slowly opening. Ben shouted.

"Look!"

There were two men inside the car, and neither of them looked very friendly. The car slid inside, and the Naitabals saw an arm extend from the car window, closing the gates behind it. The red light on the panel went off as the car disappeared from three of the screens. The car grew larger on the fourth as it came towards the camera on the bend.

Suddenly, the Naitabals were gripped by a horrible and collective instinct, and Ben put it into words.

"Quick!" he shouted. "Get out!"

They all panicked into the hall and scattered. Boff and Jayne made for the front door, hoping there was enough time to run round the house before the car came into view. Toby and Charlotte chose the side door, where they could turn quickly on to the path that led into the woods, and disappear.

Ben, undecided which way to go, stood hesitating on his own. Then another idea took hold of him. Something was telling him that just running away wouldn't help them find Mr Blake, so he ran towards the stairs instead.

The stairs went straight up from the front hall, but then turned back on themselves. Ben went up both flights and stood leaning on the top banister, looking down on the first flight. Soon after he reached the top he heard the car approaching the front of the house. He could hear everything in the hall below, but no one would be able to see him unless they came up the stairs. If they did, he would have plenty of time to slip into one of the bedrooms without being seen.

The car had already stopped, and doors were slamming. Footsteps approached the front door and came inside without stopping to ring the bell.

These men expect the house to be empty, thought Ben. Their voices came up clearly.

"I don't know about you," said the first voice, deep, with a tinge of an accent – northern, Ben thought, "but I swear I saw two kids running round the house as we came up."

"I didn't see anything." The other voice was lighter, with a London sort of flavour.

"I don't think they've gone away at all. I think our friend has told us a pack of porkies."

"We'll worry about that later. I'll check if the cleaner's been, and you see if you can find anything that looks like a blueprint – diagrams, electronic circuits, gadgets – anything. He's probably locked them in a desk or a filing cabinet somewhere – or maybe a briefcase."

"OK."

Ben heard the two sets of footsteps separate. One went along to the television room, the other to the kitchen.

Presently from a distance came the faint sounds of a search under way, drawers sliding out and in, cupboards clicking open and shut. Several minutes later the two sets of footsteps converged on the hall again.

"Found anything?" The deeper voice.

"No. Nothing's even locked. What about the cleaner?"

"The note's gone, so she must have been."

"Let's try the dining room."

Ben heard more sounds of cupboards opening and closing and furniture being moved.

Then the London voice said, "I'm going to the loo. That coffee's gone through already." The other voice said, "There's one just out by the side door. I noticed it last night."

Soon after that Ben heard a sound of cheering.

"I can't believe it!" The London voice again. "It's his briefcase! It was there on the floor!"

"It's locked."

"It's bound to be what we're looking for then, ain't it?"

"I think you might be right."

"Shall I smash it open now?"

"No. We'll give Blake the option: give us the combination, or watch us break it open. I think he'll give us the combination, don't you?"

"Yeah."

Laughter.

"Come on, we can lock the house now, and the gates."

"Yeah. We don't want anyone else snooping about."

"No."

"Let's go."

Footsteps clattered in the hall again. Ben heard the sound of keys jangling. There were murmurs in the front porch, the front door slammed, the key turned in the lock, and the car moved off.

Ben knew for certain now that Mr Blake had been kidnapped. They wanted the invention before it was patented, and they wanted to stop Mr Blake announcing it at the conference.

He ran as fast as he could down the stairs, along the corridor and into the control room. He could see the car, speeding from screen to screen, fast approaching the gates. He leaned over and threw the "Gate" switch to "Shut", and moments later found the power switch and flicked it off. The slight humming sound shrank into silence as the monitors died, and Ben was already turning to make his next move as he thought of how much time he had.

The car would be at the gates now. One of the men would be aiming the infra-red control at the gates and pressing the button. The power was off. The gates wouldn't be opening.

He had so little time. He hoped the other Naitabals wouldn't come back yet, thinking the car had gone. If they did, they might get caught. Or they'd hear the car roaring back up the drive again and scatter.

Ben knew what *he* was going to do, and he had to leave the others a message.

The man would be out of the car now, pointing the control towards the infra-red detector on the gates. The gates still wouldn't budge, and the man would be going towards them and rattling them. They'd be locked tight, and he would curse and swear.

Ben calculated that he had only about thirty seconds left. He was in the front hall now. He glanced round for anything he could write with. Chalk, crayon, a misted-up window – anything – nothing. There was a pad by the telephone, but no pen. He wished he was wearing full Naitabal battledress, but he'd left the things he needed in the Naitabal hut. But it was no good anyway. If he wrote a message like that, the men would see it. They'd know he was after them, then. They'd tear it up and catch him. Then the other Naitabals would never know what he'd done. If only he could think of a way to tell them. It would have to be a message that the men couldn't understand if they saw it. Even better if they didn't realize it *was* a message.

Now the other man would be getting out of the car to see if he could do any better with the control. He wouldn't succeed. Then they'd both be cursing and swearing and climbing back into the car and saying "Stupid damn gates!"

Ben cast round for inspiration and glimpsed only the huge bowl of fruit on the dining-room table. He wondered if anyone had ever tried writing on a window with a banana.

Then, suddenly, he had an idea. A brilliant idea! His mind was straining, thinking madly as he rushed into the dining room and grabbed oranges and apples. He spread them along the table. First an orange on its own. Then six oranges in a tight triangular group, like snooker balls. He thought ahead. There'd be enough oranges and apples and he wouldn't need any bananas at all. He needed something else.

The men would be back in the car, turning it round.

Yes! – the salt and pepper, tight together. Then an apple on its own; then another apple on its own; then six apples in a triangle. Now a gap. Nearly done. One more apple on its own, then three oranges together.

The car would be starting up the drive.

Ben stood at the door of the dining room and stole

one quick look at his handiwork, satisfied. And never even been to fruit-arranging classes, he thought. He hoped the Naitabals would find it and understand.

He ran to the first window in the sitting room and unlocked it. It opened easily. He climbed out, closed it all but a centimetre, and glanced down the drive. His thoughts of timing had been perfect. He couldn't see the car yet, but he could hear it accelerating away from the gate, the way cars do when the driver is annoyed.

He ran across the tarmac at the front of the house and dived behind one of the spherical hedges that decorated the top of the front lawn. He kept it between himself and the oncoming car, which he could hear roaring up the last stretch of the drive. It screeched to a halt at the front door and Ben adjusted his position as it drew up.

He held his breath. He hoped that they'd both get out – and, even better, leave the briefcase behind. If one man stayed in the car, there was nothing he could do . . .

He was in luck for stage one. He heard two doors opening, two sets of swear words, two sets of feet making for the front door, the sound of a key turning. He gave them another three seconds then slowly raised his head. They were both inside. He crept from his hiding place towards the car. Both doors had been flung open angrily, left open for a quick getaway. He clambered in through the nearest one, away from the house. No briefcase. He slipped between the front seats into the back. Still no briefcase. Finally, he slithered over the back seats into the estate car's big boot. There was a tartan blanket in a heap in one corner, and nothing else. He wished he could have thrown the briefcase out for the other Naitabals to find, but that was too bad. He lay down flat, hard against the back of the back seats, and pulled the blanket over himself.

Only moments later the front-door key was turning again, and the men were back. Ben felt the car rocking as they climbed in and slammed the doors.

"I know I left the power on," said a voice, aggrieved. Ben recognized the northern accent – the one with blond hair. "I looked at the screens before we came out."

The engine roared. The car lurched backwards at great speed, swerving round the flowerbed at the corner of the house.

Ben held his breath under the blanket as the car rocked forward again on its wheels and surged down the drive.

CHAPTER ELEVEN

And Then There Were Four

Toby and Charlotte ran out of the side door, swerved left, then right, on to the path that climbed through the overgrown kitchen garden, and up to the path beyond. They crouched panting behind the overgrown laurel hedge that skirted the wood above the house, looking down. Seconds later they saw the flash of a dark blue estate car cruising up the drive, and heard it slide to a stop at the front door.

"That was close!" said Charlotte. "Another few seconds and we might've been caught."

"What happened to the others?" said Toby.

"They went out the front door and across the yard. Here they come now."

Toby followed Charlotte's nod. Jayne and Boff, keeping low, were running towards them along the path behind the laurels. They caught up and dropped down beside them.

"Where's Ben?" hissed Jayne, counting heads.

"We thought he was with you!" Charlotte hissed back.

"He didn't come with us. We thought he went with you!"

Slowly, they realized that Ben hadn't escaped. None of them had seen him outside the house, although they all admitted they had been too busy running to check behind for everyone else.

"Stupid Ben," said Jayne. "Why didn't he get out with the rest of us?"

"I shouldn't worry," said Boff, not looking worried himself. "He'll just hide in the house until they've gone."

"He'll be able to hear what they say!" said Charlotte, suddenly pleased.

Jayne immediately regretted that she'd called Ben stupid. She realized that Ben was just being Ben.

"He must have stayed to listen on purpose!" said Toby.

"Good old Ben!" said Boff.

"He doesn't care about danger," said Charlotte. "Anyone who lives with the SS *Coates* on one side and HMS *Slugface* on the other has got to be brave."

"I bet he'll find out if they've done something with Mr Blake," said Jayne. "Then we can go and rescue him."

Boff was suddenly alarmed at how their voices had risen, and quietened them all down.

"The men are in the house by now," he warned. "They might hear us."

They kept quiet then, waiting for the car to drive away again. Five minutes passed, then they heard the sound of car doors banging and its engine starting. It sped off and Toby and Jayne started running back towards the kitchen garden.

"Not so fast!" hissed Boff. "They might have left someone behind, for all we know. Go quietly. Otherwise we might go barging in and give ourselves away."

Toby and Jayne put their brakes on, and Boff and Charlotte caught up with them before they started forwards again. They made their way very slowly down the steep garden path. They had started turning towards the rear of the house when they heard the sound of the car coming back again. They ducked down behind the stone wall and waited, huddled together.

The car screeched to a halt. They heard two doors open, then footsteps into the house. A minute later two doors slammed again, and the car roared away. They listened for it at the bottom of the drive, but couldn't hear much.

Later, they heard it accelerating from the gate along the straight stretch of main road.

Cedric Morgan, getting hotter and hotter, ran out into his garden and across to the fence on Charlotte's side. Her seven-year-old brother Harry was stooped by the pond, scooping things from its surface with a net, picking them out gingerly with his fingers and putting them into a matchbox that lay half open on the ground beside him.

There was no doubt at all in Cedric's mind as to who had removed the Naitabals' screwed-up letter and substituted the one saying "Hello Fat-Bang-Face". Harry. You only had to look at the scrawly writing to see that.

Cedric wanted revenge, but first he wanted the original letter. Then he could earn himself a day in the Naitabals' tree-house. His sister Doris, usually a great help when it came to bullying small people, was away at Guides camp with another gang member, Amanda Wilson. And Andy Wilson hadn't turned up yet. Cedric had to admit that it usually needed the four of them to teach Harry a lesson. Harry was well known for inflicting severe damage on his enemies in a short space of time, but only if he had his favourite weapon – a jam jar on a string.

Before moving in, therefore, Cedric made a careful visual check of the surrounding area. There was no jam jar. Harry was unarmed. All the stupid kid had was a matchbox and a little plastic net.

Cedric went down to the corner of his own garden, climbed the fence, and walked up Harry's garden towards Harry.

"Where's that letter?" he demanded.

Harry closed his matchbox, pushed it into the pocket of his short trousers and carried on dredging with his net.

"I said, where's that letter?" Cedric repeated, louder this time.

"Wot-bang letta-bang, Fat-Bang-Face," said Harry without looking up. (Harry's mastery of Naitabal language had been somewhat short-lived.)

Cedric came another two steps closer, clenching and unclenching his fists. It only needed one good shove, and the little brat would be in the pond. But Cedric wanted the letter first, while it was still dry. That letter was his passport to a stay in the Naitabal tree-house, and he wanted it – now.

"You know what letter, Harry. The one you took from my garden. The letter you put *this* in." He held up Harry's libellous scribble.

Harry frowned.

"'S'not your letta," he said, and repeated the "'S'not" because he liked the sound of it. "'S'Charlotte's letta."

"Yes, Harry. That's why I *want* it. So I can *give* it to her. *Where is it?*"

Harry pointed in the vague direction of Mr Elliott's front garden.

"In the skip-bang," he said, unconcerned.

Cedric couldn't believe his ears. It was public knowledge that anything thrown into Mr Elliott's yellow skip was as good as lost for ever. His temper, nearly at boiling point, started to bubble over.

"Right! You've asked for it! You haven't got your sister Charlotte to look after you now, have you? Or those stupid old others." He took a few more steps towards Harry to get within shoving distance.

As Cedric advanced, Harry stood up. He took the matchbox from his pocket, opened it, and tipped its contents on to one hand. He threw the empty matchbox down.

Cedric was within shoving distance now. One good push and Harry would be in the pond, covered in slime.

"If you don't go and get that letter back, I'll—" Cedric broke off and stared at the two small objects on Harry's palm. "What have you got there?" In the same second he realized exactly what Harry had been scooping from the pond.

"Drown-ded bees," said Harry. He now had one in each hand, held carefully between a finger and thumb. The stings were pointing towards Cedric.

Cedric stopped in his tracks.

"Huh!" he mocked. "They can't sting you when they're dead!"

Harry disagreed.

"Can," he said. "I stick 'em in an' squeeze 'em." To illustrate his point, he shot out both bees towards Cedric's bare arms, just missing, and Cedric leapt backwards, bleating.

The chase that followed was short, and ended with Harry's garden completely Cedric-less.

"I'll go in first," said Toby, who was nearest the house. "There's not much point all of us getting caught."

He crept away as the remaining three crouched behind the wall. They heard him calling "Ben, Ben!" in a hoarse whisper. Presently, his normal voice floated round the corner.

"The front door's locked. I can't get in."

The others rose up and surged towards the house.

"There's no one in there," said Toby. "They've all gone."

"Where's Ben?" said Charlotte.

"He must have gone as well. I called, but there was no answer."

Charlotte pushed past him.

"He must be there!" she said. She looked really worried as she rattled the front door-handle and rang the bell.

Then Jayne saw the tiny gap in the sitting-room window.

"Look!"

Moments later, Toby had slipped it wide open, and they all climbed in. They ran through the house, into all the rooms, calling for Ben, but there was no answering voice.

"I hope this isn't one of your funny jokes!" Charlotte shouted at last, into the empty air.

"I don't think Ben would joke about something like this," said Boff.

They had gathered in the hall again, and they were all looking weary.

It was Jayne who noticed the fruit.

"That's funny," she said.

"What's funny?"

"Look." She pointed. "Someone's shared all the fruit out on the dining-room table."

"It hasn't been done very fairly," Charlotte complained. "Four people have only got one fruit, yet someone's got six oranges. Someone else has got three oranges, and someone else has got six apples."

101

"That's seven people altogether," said Jayne. "There's only six of us if we include Mr Blake."

"Let's make it fairer," said Toby. He went to grab two of the oranges to start sharing them out more fairly, when Boff suddenly shouted.

"Don't! DON'T TOUCH THEM!"

Toby was so shocked, he dropped two oranges on to the floor, and went scrambling on hands and knees with Jayne to recapture them.

"Where were they?" said Boff.

"On the floor," said Toby, grinning, and clambered up.

"No! *Where were they on the table?*"

There was a maniacal urgency in Boff's voice, and his eyes were bulging behind his glasses, staring at the table.

Toby hastily put them back to make up the triangle of six again.

"What's the matter?" said Charlotte. "Boff? What's the matter?"

"It's a message," he said. "Don't you see?"

"What?"

"It's a message from Ben!"

The others turned and stared at the strange arrangement of fruit.

"No, I don't see," said Charlotte.

"Look!" Boff sounded exasperated now. "*One* orange, *six* oranges – I had a problem with the salt and pepper, but—"

"Boff!" Three voices were protesting now.

"Boff – please explain," said Charlotte.

"*Naitabal Morse!*" he said.

The others realized instantly, and kicked themselves for being so stupid.

"If you read red for oranges, and green for apples," said Boff, "then—"

"Yes, thanks, Boff," said Jayne hurriedly, and rather unkindly. "We can work it out now."

"One orange – that's 'I'," said Charlotte.

"Six oranges – that's 'N'," said Jayne.

"Salt and pepper must be two dots," said Toby. "That's 'B'."

"One apple – that's 'O'."

"And another 'O'."

"Six apples – that's 'T'."

"One apple – another 'O'."

"And three oranges – 'K'," finished Charlotte. "Oh dear, I've forgotten what the rest of them said."

"The message," said Boff, "says 'IN BOOT, OK'."

"What does that mean?" said Jayne.

"It means," said Boff patiently, "that Ben has hidden in the boot of the car and gone off with those men."

Ben had ridden in the back of an estate car once before, when his father had taken all the Naitabals ice-skating and there weren't enough seats for them all in the proper places. It had been bumpy and exciting then, but it was bumpy and uncomfortable now. This time it was worse because he had to keep as low as possible under the blanket, which meant that his head was right next to the floor. He put one hand flat under his cheek to try to soften the bumps and vibrations, but it didn't make much difference.

"Them kids, I reckon," said the ordinary voice.

"I thought Blake said they were away somewhere?"

"Very likely."

Thankfully for Ben, it wasn't a long journey. He could tell when the car slowed for the gates at the bottom of the drive, and he could tell that they turned right and went at great speed in the direction away from town. He counted a left turn, lots of wriggles and a left, lots more wriggles and another left. From the sound of the engine it felt as if they were climbing a hill, then the journey was over. The car slid to a halt on loose stones, rocking from side to side as the two men climbed out and slammed the doors. They didn't bother to lock the car, and he heard their footsteps crunching into the distance, followed by the squeaky swinging of a gate.

Slowly, very slowly and carefully, Ben started to raise his head. He kept it inside the blanket, but made a space for his eyes by holding it over his head like a shawl. He looked out first from below the level of the windows. There were no buildings nearby, so no one was looking down into the car from any windows. There were a few trees waving in the slight breeze, but no man-made features. He raised his head further. The car was parked in a gravelly yard about fifty metres from an old, dilapidated farmhouse. The house was surrounded by an overgrown hedge, and there was a single gap in it where a gate hung on a drunken post a few metres away from where Ben was hiding.

Devil's Island, he thought. Where they take all the prisoners.

Ben couldn't open the tail-gate from the inside, so he wriggled on to the back seat, still half inside his blanket. At first he was going to leave it behind, but then he thought it might come in useful, especially if he finished up spending the night in the open.

He eased open the door on the side away from the house and climbed out, pushing the door (nearly) shut with a gentle click. Crouching low, he sidled away to where the hedge was thickest and crept along its perimeter until he came to a small group of shrubs. He would have to wait until nightfall before he could go looking into the house windows – it was far too dangerous in daylight – and he tried to take his bearings. To his surprise, he found that the house was set into a hill overlooking a broad, flat valley that looked not unlike the valley he'd just left. About halfway up the hill on the far side – perhaps a mile or more away – was a large white house with green shutters, nestling in the trees. It didn't take Ben many seconds to realize that it was Mr Blake's house. *The valley looked so familiar because it was the same valley.* He rehearsed the short car journey in his mind, and everything fitted perfectly. The house across the valley was Mr Blake's house, and if he could see it from here, so could these men. They'd probably been watching it all along . . .

Ben thought about the situation. He wondered if Mr Blake was in the house somewhere, and if so, what he was doing. Was he tied up, bound and gagged? Was he unconscious? Or was he back at his house hiding somewhere, nothing to do with these men at all? Or had they taken him somewhere else altogether? He could only find out when darkness came, and in the meantime he would have to wait.

Unfortunately, Ben had less time to wait than he'd imagined. Moments later he heard the door of the house opening, and out of the wonky gate galloped a big, friendly dog. It hoovered the grass, hoovered the car, and hoovered the gravel. Then, with its big floppy tongue hanging from the side of its eager, floppy mouth, it headed in a wavy line towards where Ben was hiding.

Back in Mr Blake's dining room there was a horrible Naitabal silence as everyone realized what Ben had done.

It was only relieved when Charlotte said, "Do you think we ought to phone the police again?" and Boff answered, "I suppose we ought to try."

"It's a pity we didn't get the car number," said Toby. "The cameras are in the right position."

"We didn't have time, did we . . ." said Charlotte.

"This is a fine start to our holiday," moaned Jayne miserably. "We've only been here a day. First we lost Mr Blake, now we've lost Ben, and when the police find out, we'll all have to go home."

"Yes," said Boff. "All the more reason not to waste any more time. This is really serious. If Mr Blake *has* been kidnapped, and Ben has gone off with the kidnappers, we've no business to be messing about. I know it's brave, but he shouldn't have done it. I'll telephone the police again and tell them everything. I'll tell them to investigate, and if they start asking for names, I'll just ring off."

Looking businesslike and ultra serious, Boff rehearsed what he was going to say, then picked up the telephone.

He listened for a moment, then put the receiver down again.

"Have you changed your mind?" said the others, half hoping that he wasn't going to phone the police after all.

He turned a worried face to them.

"No," he said. "It's been cut off."

CHAPTER TWELVE

The Boy from Naitagonia

Ben dived under the blanket and pulled it tight around himself. Only seconds later he felt the powerful snuffling of the dog pushing under the edges. It had discovered the source of the lovely new smell. It gave an exultant bark, then another. It pushed and butted with its nose, barking in between, and soon found its way past the fluffy barrier. It found Ben's face and gave him enormous, liquid licks all the way from his chin to his forehead.

Ben didn't know whether to laugh or run. He couldn't help loving the dog, but the stupid thing had given him away. The men had already come running from the house, curious to know what the dog had found in the bushes. As Ben emerged from the blanket he found himself looking up at two unsmiling faces.

"It's one of them damn Naitawhotsits!" said one of them. It was the one with the London accent. He had short-cropped brown hair, so Ben immediately christened him "Flymo".

The blond, curly-headed man (Blondie, thought Ben) pulled the dog by its collar, swung it clear of Ben and pushed it away with his foot.

"Just what do you think you're doing?" he said.

The dog went sniffing across the yard, weaving from side to side, its duty done. Ben watched it for a moment, not knowing what to say. Then he remembered. He was a Naitagonian – and Naitagonians didn't understand a word of English.

He wrung his face muscles into an expression of total perplexity and said, "*Ardon-pong?*" in his best Naitabal accent.

"I said, what do you think you're doing?" Blondie repeated. He snatched the blanket from the ground and threw it angrily towards Flymo. "Put that back in the car," he ordered.

Ben found that screwing up his face for too long was making his eyes tickle. He promptly relaxed his expression into his favourite "vacant building" look – the one that made people think there was no one at home.

"*Ing on't-dang peak-song our-yung ongue-tong, tupid-song,*" he said.

"You told me Jack said they didn't speak English," Flymo called, near the car.

Ben's face lit up as he pretended to recognize the key word.

"*Ah-ang!*" he said. "Mee ... noo ... spooken ... *Eengleesh* ..."

Blondie turned to his colleague.

"We're gonna get nowhere with this one," he said.

"What do we do now, then?"

"We can't take him back, because he'll tell the other kids where we are and we'll have the whole lot of 'em over here. Even if they can't speak English, I bet they know how to grab the cops and bring them here. They've probably realized by now that Blake's missing."

Ben's face lit up again.

"*Blayk ...?*" he said. "*Blayk ...?*" He repeated the new word several times, then lifted the leaves of the nearby bush, as if searching for something.

"He wants to know where Blake is." Flymo translated.

The repeat of the magic word started Ben off again, even more excited this time. He looked behind trees, over the fence, under the car. Finally, he pointed towards the farmhouse.

"*Blayk . . .?*" he said.

The two men looked at each other.

"Well, we definitely can't take him back," said Blondie. "It's too dangerous. We'll just have to stick him in with Blake until Wednesday."

Ben started saying, "*Blayk . . . Blayk . . .* " again, and getting agitated.

The men turned, took one of Ben's arms each, and steered him firmly towards the farmhouse.

"So what do we do now?" said Charlotte. "We can't just leave poor Mr Blake in the hands of kidnappers – or whoever they are – and not do anything about it."

"Or Ben," said Jayne.

"We'll have to telephone from a public call-box," said Boff. "The only problem is, where's the nearest?"

"Why don't we just go to the police station?" said Toby.

"Because they'd insist on keeping us there, that's why," Boff explained. "They'd send us back home – and they'd make quite sure we got on the train, too."

"So it's a call-box, if we want to stay," said Jayne.

"The next problem," said Boff, "is who goes? All of us?"

"Definitely not," said Charlotte. "If we all get caught there'll be no one left to find Mr Blake – and Ben."

"So who goes?"

"I don't think any of us should go," said Charlotte, still

109

wishing they could solve the problem without outside help. "I think we should find them ourselves."

"We can't do that," said Boff. "You know we can't."

"But we're Naitabals," said Jayne.

"We've been through all this before," said Boff. "Mr Blake could be in real danger. I mean, *real* danger. And now Ben could, as well. If we don't make up our minds soon, they could both be—"

"Shut up, Boff!" said Charlotte. "Don't say it."

Jayne turned to Boff.

"I'll come with you," she said.

"Good," said Boff. "Let's go, then."

"A house would be better than a call-box," said Jayne.

"That's true," said Boff. "It'll be quicker."

The nearest house they could remember was on the main road in the direction of the town, about a quarter of a mile away, its windows right on the road.

"And we'll have a chance to get back and hide before the police arrive. Then they *can't* send us home."

Boff and Jayne climbed out of the drawing-room window and set off at a jog, while Charlotte and Toby went into the television room to unlock the gates at the bottom of the drive.

"We've got to camouflage the tree house even better," said Toby. "Then if those men come looking for us, they'll never find us."

"Let's take up more food, as well," said Charlotte. "Then we'll know we can last the whole week."

They went to the kitchen straight away and started filling carrier bags with anything they could find, but they quickly lost patience.

"I've got bad vibes," said Toby. "I want to get on with that camouflage."

"So do I," said Charlotte. "Come on."

110

Getting more anxious by the second, they set off into the woods.

Jayne and Boff were out of breath by the time they reached the gates. Boff slid them open just enough to squeeze through, then closed them again. They set off at a comfortable trot, heading towards the town, and soon reached the house on the roadside.

"It must be awfully noisy inside," said Jayne, "when the lorries go past."

They went in at the little side gates, panting heavily, and rang the bell. There was no answer.

"Oh, come on!" said Jayne, ringing it again.

There was still no answer, so Boff dropped the knocker a few times more for good measure. A quick look round the outside assured them that there was no one in the garden, either.

"Where do we go now?" said Jayne.

"We could go either way. It's pot luck."

"There's definitely another house in that direction," said Jayne, pointing the way they'd come, "about a quarter of a mile the other side of the Bay of Grass. Why don't we try that?"

"And if there's no one in, what do we do then?"

"If there's no one in, we'll just have to walk to the next house, and the next. There's bound to be someone in at one of them."

Boff agreed that the other house near to Mr Blake's was the next best try, and they set off once again as fast as their legs could bear.

Ben noticed the blond-headed man had to duck as they

111

went into the farmhouse. There were two large rooms downstairs in bad disrepair, and a kitchen. The man propelled him towards the stairs, bare of any carpet, and Ben went up. They stopped at the first door ahead of them, which was closed. The man held Ben's shoulder, turned a key in the lock with his free hand, then swung the door wide open. The other man came up behind him, carrying a black briefcase.

Ben took in the room at a single glance. There was cold linoleum covering the floor, an old wardrobe, a small table, a chair – and Mr Blake. Mr Blake was sitting on a single divan bed on the far side, smiling. He was underneath a window that had wooden shutters closed across on the inside, with a padlock attached to a metal bar. Ben worked out that the room must face across the valley.

His first priority was to stop Mr Blake talking to him in English. Even as Mr Blake was in the act of opening his mouth to speak the giveaway tongue, Ben emitted a torrent of Naitabal language and started dancing wildly into the room.

"Ing ow-kning ou-yung on't-dang peak-song Aitabal-ning anguage-ling, ut-bang all-ang is-thong ancing-dang ound-rong is-ing ust-jing o-tong top-song ou-yung iving-geng e-thong ame-geng away-ang. Es-yung?"

As soon as Mr Blake sensed that the stream was about to finish, and started opening his mouth again, Ben spewed out more nonsensical (except to Naitabals) blurb, and then started pointing and saying *"Blayk . . . Blayk . . ."* with great delight, in his rapidly improving Naitagonian accent.

At last Mr Blake, who had been looking somewhat bewildered, got the message. He turned to Blondie.

"He doesn't speak any English, you know," he said.

112

Blondie looked unimpressed.

"You don't say," he said. "I'd never have guessed."

"It does create difficulties, of course."

"I thought you said they'd gone camping for a week?"

"So they had. Where did you find this one?"

"Stowed himself in the back of my car when we visited your house just now. Thought I'd bring him up to make sure he belonged to you."

The crisis had passed.

"Yes, he's one of mine all right."

"Good. Before we decide what we're doing with him, I think we should take a look at this, don't you?" He turned, and Flymo handed him the briefcase.

Ben noticed Mr Blake's eyes dart towards it, and a worried look steal over his face.

"Yes, it's yours," said Blondie. "The one we need, I believe?"

"I don't know what you're talking about," said Mr Blake, trying to avoid eye contact.

"Look," said Blondie, with great patience, "we found this in your outside loo, so we know it's yours. And it's locked. Now, there's two ways we can open it. Either you tell us the combination for the locks, or we hit it once with a nice, sharp axe. Which would you prefer?"

Mr Blake looked beaten – and angry.

"No. Look. That briefcase contains the fruits of years of work and research which has cost me a lot of money – a lot of money. It is intellectual property to which you have no right. Merely by opening that case you are committing a criminal offence – one to add to the criminal offence of kidnapping first me, and now this poor Naitagonian child. I don't know what company you work for, but you won't get away with it. This idea will be patented and the whole world will have access to it, according to the proper rules of commerce. And I am due to announce it on Wednesday."

"A pretty speech, Mr Blake. But I beg to differ. You will not announce it on Wednesday. The ideas will not be patented – or if they are, they won't be patented by you. The combination, please?"

"I can't tell you."

"Can't?"

"Won't."

"Ned . . . Get the axe . . ."

Mr Blake hung his head. Then he said quietly. "Don't bother, *Ned*. The numbers are two-eight-nine on the left and eight-four-one on the right . . ."

Blondie smiled triumphantly and started rotating the dials on the briefcase locks.

"Thank you, Mr Blake," he said. Then he pulled the slides, fiddled with the dials, tried again – but there were no clicks. He looked up, displeased. "Those numbers don't open it."

Mr Blake frowned.

"Let me see." He took the case and tried the numbers himself, making sure they were in perfect alignment. But Mr Blake couldn't open the case, either.

"Are you having me on?" Blondie demanded.

Then a funny look came over Mr Blake's face. He glanced quickly at Ben and handed the case back to Blondie.

"I'm sorry," he said. "The numbers are three-six-one on the left and five-two-nine on the right."

Blondie's curiosity got the better of him.

"How can you remember numbers like that?"

"Oh, simple," said Mr Blake. He waved the irritating question aside. "There are only seven prime numbers whose squares have three digits, and only two of those—"

114

"Sorry I asked," interrupted Blondie, who was really only interested in the contents of the briefcase. There were two clicks as the locks snapped open, and he lifted the lid. The new look of triumph fell from his face as he scooped his hand into the almost-empty case and held up five blank envelopes.

"What are these?" he demanded.

Mr Blake didn't need to look. He knew already.

"I'm afraid," he said, "it's the wrong briefcase . . ."

"What?"

Mr Blake shrugged.

"I'm sorry," he repeated. "It's the wrong briefcase." Then he noticed that Blondie was looking closely inside one of the envelopes, and added, "Please don't say what they are – they're a surprise for our Naitagonian visitors."

"I thought you said they don't understand English."

"They don't. But I think you'll agree that those pieces of paper would be understood in any language."

Now Blondie's tone was short and sharp.

"Where's the right briefcase?"

Mr Blake sighed.

"I'll tell you the truth if you'll promise me that no harm will come to these children."

"No harm will come to them. But we can't take this one back yet, can we? Not until after Wednesday? He'd tell the others, and they'd find some way of telling someone to dial nine-nine-nine."

"Yes, that is a point," said Mr Blake.

"*I don't want to go back*," said Ben in Naitabal language, looking up at Blondie. "*I want to stay here and rescue Mr Blake*."

"Bless him," murmured Mr Blake to the men. "He tries so hard."

"Do you speak this – this . . . Naitagonian?" said Blondie.

"Good gracious, no," said Mr Blake truthfully. "I don't understand a word of it. He sensed we were talking about him."

"Well, how do you communicate, then?"

Mr Blake's mind started to go blank until he noticed Ben fingering the Naitabal torch in his pocket and pulling meaningful faces.

"Ah!" he said, catching on. "That's the amazing thing about Naitagonian. It's like . . . it's like a – a cross between Egyptian and Chinese. I can't *speak* it, and I don't understand the spoken word, but I know the sign language."

Mr Blake pulled out the borrowed Naitabal torch that was still in his pocket from his walk the night before. He flashed it a few times at random in red, green and white.

"What do you mean, sign language?"

"It's . . . it's like deaf and dumb language, but they do it with different-coloured lights. And it involves mathematics as well," Mr Blake went on, making it up as he went. "For instance," – demonstrating – "*red, green, wiggle* means you've got to pay someone some money, and *green, red-red-red* means everything's fine, and *white-white, white-white, white-white-white* means there's a good programme on the television."

Ben grinned inside, but Blondie was looking suspicious.

"You're having me on," he said.

"No, really," said Mr Blake. "Tell me to ask him something, and I'll get an answer for you."

Blondie thought for a moment.

"Ask him where his friends are."

Ben put on his vacant-building expression, and Mr Blake started flashing the torch. He spelt out, "*This man*

116

is an idiot." Ben smiled and nodded at the right moment and flashed back, "*Yes. Me help you escape.*"

"What did he say?" said Blondie.

"He said 'They're in the house'," lied Mr Blake.

"Ask him why we didn't see them when we went there just now."

Mr Blake flashed, "*Vital solve clues by Wednesday*" which made Ben realize that the situation was still serious. He paused for a moment to think, then replied, "*Why?*"

"He said 'Pardon?'," explained Mr Blake. "I'll have to ask that one again," He signalled, "*I buried wrong case*" and Ben answered, "*First clue missing. Are five envelopes clues?*" Mr Blake flashed "*No. Treasure. My copy clues buried with other case,*" and Ben came back with "*Cedric got ours.*"

"What was all that about?" said Blondie.

"I'm sorry – I'm a bit rusty on some of the signs. I had to repeat a few things. He said they saw the strange car coming, and hid. But he wanted to find me, so he decided to get in the car."

"Well, now you can tell him if I don't get the briefcase my boss is after, they'll never see Naitagonia again."

Ben took this cue to start saying, "*Naitagonia . . . Naitagonia . . .*" and laughing and clapping his hands. He was also dying to know what was in the envelopes that would be recognized in any language, but he stuck faithfully to his role of complete foreigner, understanding nothing.

Mr Blake looked serious.

"These children are refugees from a country that has been embroiled in civil war since the break-up of—"

"I don't care," said Blondie, rudely interrupting. "I want that briefcase, and I want it before Wednesday. And

117

if I don't get it before Wednesday, these little ruffians can say 'Goodbye, Naitagonia'. Understand?"

"Your threats against these children are useless – I can't get my hands on the briefcase myself."

"Why not?"

"It's simple. You see, I posted it to myself in Cardiff, care of the conference. The only person who can claim it is me."

Blondie sneered.

"I don't believe you. You're bluffing. You've hidden it in the house or grounds somewhere, and we're going to turn the place inside out until we find it. So the quicker you tell us, the nicer your house will be, if you ever get back to it."

"I told you – I posted it."

Ben started flashing furiously, and Mr Blake read the message: "*Have you really posted it?*"

"What's the kid saying?"

"He wants to know what we're arguing about." Mr Blake flashed back, "*No. Buried in woods. Can't remember where. Too tricky. Clues vital. Find.*" and said to Blondie, "I've told him not to worry, and that he'll soon be back with his friends."

"Good." He nodded to his accomplice. "Shut the kid in the other room. We'll leave Ned in charge. You and I are going souvenir-hunting."

Minutes later, the car was speeding back through the lanes, down the hill towards the main road.

CHAPTER THIRTEEN

Red-Green-Red

Ben was steered firmly out of Mr Blake's room and into the one next door. The man called Ned, who looked harmless and stupid, closed the door and locked it. His voice came through the wood.

"Don't try jumpin' out of the window. It's a long way up and I'm not scrapin' you off the concrete." Presently his footsteps receded down the stairs.

Ben had almost answered back in English. It was an automatic reaction, but he had managed to stop himself in time. It would have been disastrous to give himself away now, after all his hard work.

He surveyed the room. It was even worse than the one Mr Blake was in. It had bare floorboards, a bed with a stained mattress, one old fluffy blanket, and no other furniture at all. Presently Ned came back. He put an empty bucket in the corner and dropped a roll of loo paper next to it.

"That'll stop you botherin' me," he said, and disappeared again.

Ben screwed up his nose. Well, at least he hadn't had much to drink lately, he thought, and hoped he wouldn't need to use it.

The room was in a terrible state. Two of the floorboards were loose, plaster had fallen off the walls in great chunks, and most of them were still lying where they had fallen. Even worse, half the ceiling was hanging dangerously low in the middle and looked as if it might collapse if a spider hung from it. Through its holes he could see the sagging timbers of the floor above.

He went to the window, avoiding the middle of the room, and looked down. It was a long way to the ground, and he didn't have the strength to open the window anyway – it had been painted over so many times it must have been shut for years. He might be able to smash the glass, but there wasn't anything to smash it with – except the bucket.

Ben's spirits rose briefly at the thought, then fell again. If he smashed the window, the stupid Ned would come running up to see what the noise was. He wouldn't even have time to knock out the treacherous shards of glass before he was caught. There was no chance that way.

He looked across the valley. The light was already failing fast. He could still see Blake Island with Naitagonia clustered round it like a huge shawl, protecting it. In between he could see bits of the main road here and there through the gaps in the trees and hedges. It was a long way away, but he could make out two people running along. Small people. Small enough to look like—

Ben's heart nearly stopped. He squeezed his nose against the window, trying to see more clearly, but it only made the glass mist up and he had to move to a clear part. The figures had disappeared behind a hedge now, jogging. They came out the other side, still running, at least a mile along the road from Mr Blake's house. They were wearing the right *colours* for Jayne and Boff, but other than that he couldn't really make out any detail at all. Now they had stopped at a house. He could just see them standing against the white door, tiny in the distance.

They were there for several minutes, but Ben couldn't see if the door opened. Now they were turning and coming back down the path.

Ben's heart thumped again as he suddenly remembered the Naitabal torch that was still in his pocket. Hands shaking, fingers fumbling, he pulled it out. He pointed it through the window and began shifting the coloured lenses and pressing the button.

Red-green-red. Red-green-red. Red-green-red . . .

"I don't believe it!" said Jayne.

She and Boff were standing at the door of the third house they had tried and were getting no answer there, either.

"Where is everybody?" said Boff. "Is it market day in town, or something?"

"I don't know, but this is getting past the joke stage."

"Come on," said Boff. "We'll have to try the next one – we'll have to."

"I can't. My legs have gone numb."

"Mine went numb ages ago. Anyway, that means you can't feel any pain, doesn't it?"

"I can feel pain round the edges where the numb finishes," Jayne complained, half-joking.

"Come on. This is for Ben, remember, and Mr Blake. They might be putting up with a lot more than we are."

"After all, we are Naitabals," said Jayne, reassuring herself. "And Naitabals never give up."

"Even," added Boff drily, "when their legs are numb with painful edges . . ."

They set off again, still running in the direction that led away from town. They had travelled this way over a mile now, and they could already see their fourth target another quarter of a mile away. Mr Blake's house had shrivelled alarmingly into the distance, and now it was hidden by the hedges that towered over them at the roadside.

They reached the next house and struggled up the uneven path.

"I feel as if I'm running in golden syrup," said Jayne. In spite of this handicap, she got to the white door first. She leaned on the bell and dropped the knocker several times. She closed her eyes for a second, red-faced and panting from the run, then crossed both sets of fingers and looked towards the sky.

"Please be in!" she said. "Please! Please let someone be in!"

They waited, but no sound came from inside.

"Not even a dog at this one!" said Boff bitterly. He was normally ultra-calm, but now he hammered the knocker in a fury until his hand was sore. He looked through the front window. "Look! There's a telephone, just sitting doing nothing, and there's no way we can get to it!"

There was still no response, so they turned and retraced their footsteps down the path.

"I can't believe four houses in a row can have no one in," Boff complained. "It's almost as if the laws of probability are against us."

They stood at the gate, facing the road, trying to decide what to do next.

"If we go back towards Mr Blake's," said Jayne, "we'll have to go a mile and a half just to reach the first house again. And if we go to the right, we'll be getting even further away."

"What about up there?" said Boff. He pointed ahead of them, where they could see intriguing fragments of lanes winding through the hills, with little houses scattered at odd intervals in the distance.

"They're miles away," said Jayne.

"There's smoke coming out of one of the chimneys. There's bound to be someone there."

"Not knowing *our* luck. They probably went out and left the house on fire."

"And it's uphill all the way," said Boff, not relishing a climb.

They both took deep breaths and decided to carry on to the right. But as they turned, Jane noticed something out of the corner of her eye. She stopped dead in her tracks and squinted towards the tiny house where it had come from. It was so faint it took her a few moments to find it again.

"Look!" she said.

Boff looked.

"What?"

"There! You see that house on the ridge to the left?"

"Yes. What about it?"

"Look!"

"Don't keep saying 'Look!'. I'm already looking. It would help if you told me what I'm looking *for*."

"Can't you see the light flashing? Look!"

"You said it again!" Boff screwed up his eyes behind his glasses. The sun was already halfway below the hills. He stared at the house. He *could* see something – a light flashing in one of the dark windows. But it was so weak and pathetic he was surprised Jayne had noticed it at all.

Now Jayne was gripping his arm.

"Boff!" she screamed. "It's red-green-red! *It's red-green-red*, Boff!"

"It can't be!"

"It is! It is! Look! It must be Ben! It *must* be Ben!"

"Quick, where's your torch?"

"I gave mine to Mr Blake. Yours is in your belt."

But Jayne had pulled it out even before Boff's hand had started moving. She pointed it towards the house on the distant ridge. "*Green, red-red-red*," she signalled. "*Green, red-red-red*."

The reply, so faint they could hardly see it, came seconds later: "*Green-green-green-green-green-green, green, red-red-red-red-red-red, red . . .* "

But before they had a chance to see the rest of the new message, they heard a car coming along the road, fast. They automatically stood away from the verge, but as the car whipped past them it made the air sway with the force, and Jayne's voice cut through the noise.

"That was the men!"

The occupants of the car had obviously seen them as well. A hundred metres further down the road the car's brake lights came on, and the car snaked to a halt.

"Come on!" said Boff. He grabbed Jayne's arm and they ran back up the path. At the same moment the front door of the house opened and an old man, sleepy-eyed, unshaven and half dressed, swayed on the doorstep.

"That you knockin'?" he said.

"Yes," said Boff, taken by surprise.

Jayne looked back. She could see the car through the gaps in the hedgerow that bordered the main road.

"I was in bed. You was knockin' so 'ard I thought I'd better come down."

"We're really sorry to disturb you," Boff apologized.

"Not another accident, is it? This road's terrible for accidents."

They heard a car door slam, rapid footsteps on the road.

"No, there's no accident," said Boff. "We just

124

wondered if we could use your telephone?"

Jayne's spirits sank. A few minutes before, she had wanted to find a telephone more than anything. First, Mr Blake being lost, then Ben. It was almost more than she could bear. But now they knew where Ben was – and probably Mr Blake as well – and she didn't want the police interfering. The moment the police were told anything, the Naitabals would all be packed off home, and Ben would be in big trouble for going off in a stranger's car.

"Course you can! What's the trouble?"

"We've come from Darkwood House—" Boff began.

Jayne clutched at his elbow.

"Boff—" she started to interrupt in alarm, pulling him, not wanting him to call the police. Seconds later she realized that Boff was still Boff – his quick brain was way ahead of hers.

"—I'm afraid our telephone's out of order, and we wondered if we could phone the engineers to get it fixed?"

"Course you can! Course you can! Come in!"

Jayne relaxed her frantic grip on Boff's elbow and grinned with huge relief. Boff didn't want to call the police, either – not now they'd found Ben!

As they stepped into the house they heard the car door slam again, followed by the sound of the car moving off at speed.

Boff called the engineers, then he and Jayne thanked the man profusely.

"Is it all right to go back across your fields?" Boff asked him.

"Course it is! Course it is!" The man showed them down his garden, fetched some step-ladders so they could climb his fence, and waved them off.

125

"Come on!" said Boff, leading across the field. "We don't need the police! Not now we know where Ben is!"

"And Mr Blake!" panted Jayne.

They ran towards the woods ahead of them which sprawled on the hillside for over a mile, merging with the distant woods of Naitagonia away to their right.

Suddenly their legs weren't tired any more.

At about the time when Ben was being frog-marched into the farmhouse, having been discovered by the dog, Toby was fetching the bamboo pole to unlock the tree-house and Charlotte was making sure that any traces of their activities on the ground were well and truly hidden.

Five minutes later, all the extra food they had collected was stowed safely inside. They stood below now, looking up, trying to decide where they needed extra camouflage.

"It just needs a bit under the floor, really," said Charlotte. "That's the only place it shows."

"That's what I thought," said Toby. "We can get ivy from that tree" – pointing – "and weave it through the ivy on ours. That'll hide the floor."

They set to work immediately, gathering thick bunches of ivy from the nearby tree, hauling them up their own, and weaving them into the surrounding ivy and underneath the floor.

"Leave enough space for the trap-door to open," Charlotte reminded him.

They tied more pieces to the trap-door with string so that the greenery overlapped when it was shut. Eventually they rolled up the rope-ladder, closed the trap-door and stood admiring their handiwork.

"You'd never know it was there," said Charlotte, pleased.

Toby seemed satisfied as well, and they voted to go inside the Naitabal hut, close it up, and wait for the others.

"I hope Ben's all right," said Charlotte in a hushed voice when they were safely inside. "I hope he hasn't done anything silly."

"Ben'll be OK," said Toby. "He always is. And why are you whispering?"

"Well, it's a fat lot of use being totally hidden by ivy if people can hear two idiots talking, isn't it?"

"Oh – yeah," said Toby, dropping his voice to match. "Good thinking."

"I wonder if Boff and Jayne have phoned the police yet? I haven't heard any sirens."

"No. We'll just have to wait, I suppose."

Ben kept signalling, *red-green-red, red-green-red*, narrowing his eyes, hoping they'd see: *red-green-red, red-green-red*, over and over again, pointing his torch as steadily as he could.

He could hardly believe his luck when he saw it. It was faint and fragile, like a pinprick of a star thousands of light-years away, a tiny spark of hope. It was answering, *green, red-red-red, green, red-red-red*.

"OK!" Ben said aloud, forgetting himself. "They're saying OK!"

They'd seen his signal and understood.

The light from their torch was so minute, Ben wasn't confident of reading long messages – it must be the same for them, he thought. It would be easier later, when it was dark.

He started signalling again, T, O, N, I, G, H, T, but halfway through a car sped past the figures on the road

– it looked like the men's estate car. The two Naitabals turned and disappeared inside the house. Ben didn't see the car or the figures again.

As the light slowly faded from the sky, Ben had to face a new dilemma. Boff and Jayne had seen him – if it was Boff and Jayne – but he still needed to tell them how urgent it was to solve the clues and find the buried briefcase. If he tried to attract their attention too early, they might not be looking. His torch batteries might run down. But if he didn't flash until later, they might lose sight of the house in the darkness and stand where they couldn't see it. Then they'd never get the message.

Ben decided on a compromise. As soon as it was really dark, he would send three red-green-reds every three minutes.

Boff and Jayne reached the edge of the woods and stopped for a short rest as the sun finally dropped behind the hills.

"It'll be dark soon," panted Boff. "I vote we keep going."

"I'm tired," said Jayne. "I need a rest."

"We should go as far as we can while it's still light. While we can still see the house where Ben is. Then we can start signalling again."

"Shouldn't we warn the others about the men coming back?"

"I don't think it matters. Anyway, the men'll be there by now. Even if they go into the woods, they'll never find the tree-house – not if Toby and Charlotte have done a good job on that extra camouflage. Why would they look for us anyway? If they *have* caught Ben, I'm sure they don't want another four cluttering up their plans."

"No. But Toby and Charlotte'll be wondering where we've got to. They'll be worried when it gets dark."

"They know we've got a torch. Anyway, it's more important that we contact Ben first."

With some of their breath back, they ran on, glancing to their right every few seconds to make sure Ben's house was still visible. Soon the trees grew thicker, the ground climbed higher, and the treetops started getting in the way.

"We'd better stop now," said Boff. "I don't think we'll get many gaps further on."

They still had a good view of where the house was, but the scenery was darkening rapidly. Before long, the landscape had lost its colour, and everything was in different shades of grey. Then the hedges and trees slowly merged into the fields. Presently, all they could see was black hills on the horizon and patches of dark, moonless sky in the trees above them.

"I'll try a signal," said Jayne. She took the torch from Boff. "Shall I just red-green-red?"

Boff nodded in the darkness and added, "Yes," keeping his eyes firmly on the place where they had last seen Ben's house.

Jayne began.

Red-green-red. Red-green-red.

"Just do it once every now and again," said Boff. "He'll see it if he's looking this way."

It wasn't long before the answer came.

Dot, red-red-red-red-red. Green, red-red-red.

"AM OK," translated Boff.

Dot-dot, red-red-red-red, dot, red-red-red, dash, green, red-red-red.

"BLAKE OK."

129

"I'll signal 'good'," said Jayne, "so he knows we're listening."

"Looking," corrected Boff.

Jayne signalled her reply, and then the exchanges grew longer and more confident. Ben's first wiggle came with the next message:

"VITAL YOU SOLVE CLUES."

"Those wiggles were easy to see," said Jayne, then replied "WHY?" with some big wiggles of her own, moving the torch from side to side as far as her arms would reach.

"FIND BURIED BRIEFCASE."

"WHY?"

"VITAL TO BLAKE. HIDE BRIEFCASE FROM MEN."

"WHAT IS IN IT?"

But it was a question that was never answered. Without any warning, there were no more flashes from Ben.

"What's happened?" said Jayne. She repeated her last Naitabal Morse message, then again, then for a fourth time. But nothing came in reply.

"It's worrying," said Boff. "I hope he's all right."

"I hope the men haven't found him and taken his torch away."

Boff sounded grim as he stared into the blackness.

"I just hope that's all they *have* done," he said.

CHAPTER FOURTEEN

Housewrecked

Boff and Jayne waited for another fifteen minutes, but there were no more messages from Ben. They signalled a few times themselves, red-green-red, at intervals, but there was still no response.

"Come on," said Jayne. "Charlotte and Toby will be really worried if we don't get back soon."

Boff stirred in the darkness and didn't argue.

As they turned and moved off, something else caught Jayne's eye, and she touched Boff's arm to hold him back.

"Look!"

Over to their left and slightly behind they could see an orange glow. It shone through a rectangular window and threw up silhouettes of the jagged, broken walls that surrounded it.

"It's Ruin Island!" said Boff. "Where Annie lives."

Charlotte and Toby were temporarily forgotten as Jayne said, "Shall we go and see her? She might know something about the house where Ben is."

"We could go and look," said Boff, "but she's a bit weird. I don't think we should tell her anything."

"No," said Jayne. "Perhaps not. I've seen her in the distance once or twice in Naitagonia. I think she's been watching us."

They made their way stealthily to the glow of the ruined house until they could see through the hole that used to be a window. Annie was sitting in a deckchair, reading. The open fire at her feet spread a warm glow all around the interior of the roofless, derelict house.

"Come in!" she called.

Jayne and Boff, proud of their silent approach, were shocked.

"S-sorry," Boff stuttered. "We just wanted to see what your house was like."

"Come in, come in. I won't turn you into frogs."

They moved forward slowly and stood on a low ledge that used to be a doorway.

"We've got to get back," said Jayne, "or the others will be worried."

"You know where to find me now," she said, looking up at them, "if you're in trouble."

"Yes. Thank you."

They turned to leave.

"You be careful. Stick to the path you were following and you can't go far wrong."

"How did you—?"

Annie smiled a ghostly smile in the orange glow.

"I don't miss much of what goes on in these woods," she said, and slowly closed one eye.

Boff and Jayne didn't know what else to say. They retraced their steps as quickly as torchlight would allow.

When they had rejoined their path, Jayne said, "Did you hear that?" and Boff said, "What?"

Jayne strained her ears, listening.

"I thought – no, it couldn't have been."

"You thought what?"

"I – I thought I heard a telephone ringing – but I couldn't have, could I?"

"No," said Boff, dismissing it.

While their minds turned over and over all the things that might have happened to Ben, their feet picked their way homeward through the black, wild woods. They only used the torch when they needed to negotiate obstacles like barbed-wire fences or wide ditches, and to check around them for eyes that might be glowing in the dark, watching them. But they saw no one and heard nothing. After twenty minutes and a few false trails they found themselves standing beneath the newly camouflaged Naitabal hut, black and silent.

Before either of them spoke, Jayne flashed the torch around once more to make sure no one had followed them. Then she called softly in Naitabal language.

"Arlotte-chang, it's-ing us-ung! Oby-tong!"

Within two seconds the trap-door sprang open, and Jayne's torch picked out the white, ghostly faces of Charlotte and Toby above.

"Thank goodness!" said Charlotte. "We were getting worried!"

The rope-ladder was lowered, Jayne and Boff climbed up it as quickly as they could, and everything was secured again. The four sat in a circle, a single torch shining up in the middle, throwing hideous shadows on the walls around them.

They talked in whispers.

"Did you phone the police?" said Charlotte. "We heard a car going up Mr Blake's drive."

"No," said Boff. "But we know where Ben and Mr Blake are."

"That's fantastic!"

With Jayne's help, Boff recounted everything that had happened to them, starting with their failure to contact the police, describing the episode with the men's car, and ending with the messages from Ben and the brief encounter with Ruins Annie.

"Basically," Boff concluded, "we've got to finish solving the clues. They lead us to the buried briefcase, but we don't know what's in it. Ben said it's vital for Mr Blake that we find it, but he didn't say why."

"He didn't have time," said Jayne, explaining how the torch flashing had stopped rather abruptly. "But he said to make sure those men don't get hold of it."

Charlotte was really worried for Ben now. She quizzed Boff and Jayne for every detail, but they had already told them everything they knew.

"I bet that's why the men are in the house now," said Toby, joining in for the first time. "Looking for the briefcase."

"We don't know they're at the house," said Charlotte.

"No, but we heard a car come up. And we've been dead quiet, and we haven't heard it going down."

"What I want to know," said Jayne, "is how we're going to solve the rest of these clues. We can't exactly go running and screaming round the woods with those men down there. They've already got Ben, so I don't suppose another four would make much difference."

"It's late," said Charlotte, suppressing a yawn and making her eyes water. "We'll have to sleep on it." She glanced at Boff for approval, but Boff had suddenly gone into one of his deep-thought trances. She nudged the others, and the three of them watched Boff in silence, fascinated.

Seconds later, Boff stirred again.

"Here it comes!" said Jayne. "A Boff idea!"

They waited a little longer, then Boff spoke.

"The only way we can avoid the men," he said slowly, "is to switch to being nocturnal."

The spooky shadows of Toby's face broke into a broad grin in the dim torchlight.

"You mean sleep during the day?" he said eagerly.

"Yes, Toby," said Boff. "I thought you'd like that idea."

"And do all our clue-solving at night?" said Charlotte.

"That's it," said Boff.

"Brilliant!"

"What's more," Boff continued, "we can lock the gates when we know the men have gone – make it difficult for them to come to the house. And if they come looking for us in the woods, all they'll find is a perfectly silent place with no one in it at all."

"Because we'll all be asleep in here," said Toby, still grinning.

"As long as you don't snore and give the game away," said Jayne accusingly.

"Or any of us, for that matter," said Charlotte.

"So I suggest we get a couple of hours' sleep now," said Boff, "and get up at about one o'clock in the morning."

"When do we eat?" said Jayne. "I'm starving."

"We can light a fire at one o'clock in the morning and have a hot meal," said Charlotte. "But we'll have to light it away from the Naitabal hut so no one puts two and two together."

"We could do it in Mr Blake's house," said Toby, but regretted his suggestion almost immediately.

"Toby!" said Jayne and Charlotte together, followed by Charlotte's "Wash your mouth out with vinegar, and sing the Naitabal Earth Song three times backwards! As if Naitabals would even *think* of cooking in a house when there's a dark wood and an open fire!"

"Shame on you!" echoed Jayne, and Boff stared at Toby over his spectacles as if checking to see if he had suddenly lost his sanity.

Then they tried to settle down for a couple of hours' sleep. Even as they drifted into slumber, they heard the sound of a car leaving Mr Blake's house.

When they woke up, they would have midnight Naitagonia to themselves.

It was already dark at the farmhouse. The man called Ned, who had been assigned to stay and look after Mr Blake and Ben, was bored. He knew the place had been specially rented to keep an eye on Blake's house, but it was very sparsely furnished. There was no television to while away the time, no radio, no books, and not much in the way of food.

Three quarters of an hour after his colleagues had departed, he wandered outside to look at the stars. He didn't know what any of them were called, but they were nice to look at in the country, and there was always the chance of seeing a shooting star or a UFO.

When he got outside he saw a UFO straight away. It wasn't in the sky, though, and it wasn't flying. It was an Unidentified Flashing Object. It appeared in the woods on the far horizon, and it was flashing red, white and green. It came in short spasms, stopped for a while, then flashed again. Ned was intrigued. Had it already landed? He scratched his head and looked back towards the farmhouse as if seeking a second opinion. As he did so, he discovered that the UFO was not confined to the distant hill. There was another one in the farmhouse window.

It dawned on Ned's brain that the Unidentified Flashing Objects were talking to each other. The kid was messing around with his torch, signalling to his Naitagonian friends in the woods opposite.

He turned on his heel and rushed back into the house and up the stairs.

"What d'you fink you're doing?" he said.

Ben opened his eyes. He had heard the footsteps coming up the stairs and the door being unlocked. He had already pushed the Naitabal torch into his pocket, swooned on to the bed and pretended to be asleep. But it was too late. The little man grabbed the torch from Ben's pocket and went away, locking the door again.

Ben jumped up and steered himself back towards the window. The Naitabal torch across the valley signalled "WHAT IS IN IT?" a few times more, then stopped. A little while afterwards there came *red-green-red* at short intervals, until the signals stopped altogether.

Ben went to the door and switched on the light. He had to escape somehow, but he didn't know how. It was pitch black outside the window, but he remembered the distance to the ground, and the problem with breaking the glass. He could never get out that way. He tried the door. It was definitely locked. That left the ceiling and the floor.

Ben looked through the gaping hole where the ceiling hung precariously into the room. It was a hole he could climb through – into the attic, he thought – but it looked far too dangerous, even for Ben. He could jump up and reach the beams that sagged down, but there was every chance that the whole lot would come down on top of him. The house was literally falling to pieces.

That left the floor. Several of the floorboards were completely loose, as if they'd been taken up to hide something, or perhaps to do repairs that never got finished. He lifted them out one by one, but could see only dust and the boards of the ceiling underneath. He could kick his way through, but the man would just catch him in the room below.

Ben sat on the bed again. He *had* to escape, he *had* to. He owed it to the other Naitabals. He'd found out where the men were keeping Mr Blake, and he'd got his message through. Now, mission accomplished, he wanted to help them solve the other clues and find the buried briefcase.

His eyes roamed the door, the window, the floor, the ceiling. Perhaps he should risk climbing through the ceiling after all. The worst that could happen was ...

Suddenly Ben had an idea. A brilliant idea, though he said so himself. He thought it through. Yes, it would work, he was sure it would work ... It would have to be done now, before the other men got back. It could only work if the man Ned was in the house by himself ...

Carefully, Ben lifted one of the loose floorboards. With great care and effort, standing near the corner behind the door, he worked its far end into the hole in the ceiling. He pushed it in a long way, making sure he could still reach the end sticking out. Then he twisted it on to its edge so that it was wedged and wouldn't snap when he put his weight on it.

Ben flung himself on to the end, using it as a lever, and pulled downwards with all his weight. He knew it was dangerous, but there was no changing his mind, now. What if he was hit on the head with a chunk of plaster, or a heavy beam? Suddenly, it was too late to worry. There was a tremendous creaking groan, and seconds later the whole of the ceiling, which had hung so precariously for so long, came crashing down into the room – beams, laths, plaster, the floor above, and everything. It made a terrible noise, louder than the loudest crash of thunder he'd ever heard in his life.

The room was engulfed with filthy black and white dust at the same moment as the light went out. Ben, from the relative safety of his corner behind the door, automatically turned his head away from the choking atmosphere, trying to breathe.

He heard Mr Blake shouting in panic, and footsteps pounding up the stairs. Somewhere, the dog was barking. There was a frantic conversation through the next door, then the sound of the key in his own lock. As the door opened, light from the corridor flooded the room, and Ben saw, from under a protective slab of ceiling, the devastation he had caused. Ned rushed in, shouting.

"Are you under there, mate? Are you under there?"

Ned knelt down and started dragging rubble from the huge heap in the middle of the floor, and Ben seized his chance. He whizzed round the door, slammed it shut and locked the man inside.

Out on the landing, Ben looked up. There was a trap door to the loft, and it was bolted. Ben felt pleased: that meant the man wouldn't be able to get out that way, through the loft. Mr Blake was shouting anxiously, hammering on his door, and now Ned started shouting, hammering on *his* door and calling Ben names.

Mr Blake's door was firmly locked with no key in sight.

"Blayk!" called Ben through the keyhole.

"Are you all right?" Mr Blake's voice, very relieved.

"Me OK," said Ben, sticking to his Naitagonian accent. He didn't want to give the game away to Ned.

"You get away!" shouted Mr Blake. "Don't worry about me! Find the briefcase. Remember two-eight-nine and eight-four-one."

Ben repeated the numbers, but wasn't confident he'd remember them.

"If you can't," said Mr Blake, "just remember it's two *prime* numbers *squared* – the only two that have an eight in. Can you remember that? Tell Boff. Now go!"

Ben didn't wait any longer. He knew that the best thing he could do for Mr Blake was to escape and help the others. If he hung around looking for the key to Mr Blake's room, the other men might return and catch him.

His torch was on a table downstairs. He grabbed it and ran outside, trying hard to remember what the surrounding countryside was like. Was it better to go straight across the fields and fences, or to follow the road? Going by road would be easier, but further, and there was a good chance of meeting the men on their way back. Anyway, he was a Naitabal – and Naitabals didn't use roads unless they really had to.

Ben scrambled over the low stone wall and stopped to glance back at the house. He could see Mr Blake silhouetted between the half-open shutters of the room where he was locked up. There was something wrong with the image, but Ben didn't know what. Next door to Mr Blake, Ned was banging on the window.

Ben Tuffoudini, the world's most famous escape artist, turned in the darkness and headed in the direction of Blake Island. He had to cross the dangerous Arrow Straits, circumnavigate the Barbary Coast, cross the treacherous Sea of Grass, and enter the wilds of Naitagonia. There were no lights to tell him exactly where it was, but it didn't matter. He was a secret agent, working for the British government. His speciality was finding black wine gums in coal mines at midnight . . .

An hour later he was standing under the Naitabal hut, tired and scratched and slightly damp. He abandoned his dual personalities of Ben Tuffoudini and secret agent and started being an owl instead.

CHAPTER FIFTEEN

Owls-ong

"Charlotte!"

The word was whispered almost soundlessly in her ear, and she snapped awake. It was Jayne's voice next to her in the blackness, and Jayne's hot breath on her cheek.

"Is it one o'clock already?"

"No! But there's an owl under the hut!"

Jayne could sense Charlotte's face screwing up, sucking in air ready to complain.

"Did you wake me up just to—"

"Sshh!"

They both listened. It wasn't the sound of an owl this time, more like gas escaping from a drink can.

"Ffssss!"

"There!" whispered Jayne.

"That's not an owl, stupid, that's a snake!" hissed Charlotte, sounding like one herself.

There was the low hoot of an owl then, followed by the "Ffssss!" sound again.

"It's an owl with a puncture!" breathed Charlotte.

They both started giggling, hurting their ribs, because they had to giggle without making any noise.

This time the owl hoot was followed by a whispered "Hoy!" and Jayne and Charlotte sat up in their sleeping-bags.

"A *talking* owl with a puncture!" Charlotte spluttered, and set them off again.

When their convulsions subsided, Jayne said, "It sounds like Ben!"

Seconds later they were easing open the trap-door a few centimetres, peering through the edges of the ivy to make sure it was true. Standing below, shining his torch on to his own face, was Ben.

"It *is* Ben!" they chorused, this time loud enough to wake Boff and Toby.

A few minutes later Ben was inside the tree-house, warming himself up in his sleeping-bag.

"You're all covered in dust and cobwebs," Jayne remarked, picking some out of his hair. "You look like Mr Elliott!"

Ben sat up with his back propped against the wall while the others slithered round to listen to his story. He told them everything, starting with his hiding in the men's car. He explained how he had managed to speak to Mr Blake in front of the men by using Naitagonian Flash Language ("He must mean Naitabal Morse," put in Boff), and finished with the story of the housewreck and his escape.

"They're trying to pinch Mr Blake's invention!" he said. "But I couldn't get Mr Blake out," he added, apologizing. "I couldn't see the key anywhere, and I didn't want to stay too long in case the other men came back."

The others congratulated him and related their own adventures.

Ben grinned at Charlotte and Toby. "Your extra camouflage was brilliant – it took me ages to find the tree!" Then he reminded them again of the urgency of finding the briefcase.

"I don't really understand about the briefcase," said Jayne.

"Well," said Ben, "Mr Blake put five envelopes in a briefcase and buried it somewhere – that was the treasure for our treasure hunt . . ."

"One envelope each," said Toby, smiling.

". . . But he had *another* briefcase with the plans for his invention and the patent, and the conference—"

"The Police Conference on Wednesday," put in Boff.

". . . but he put a copy of the clues in it as well, and—"

"And he promised to leave a copy of the first clue for us," said Jayne.

"But he couldn't," Ben continued, "because the men took him away. They didn't know about the briefcase at first, but they found it when I was hiding in the house and they made him open it, but it was the wrong one."

"What do you mean, it was the wrong one?" said Charlotte.

Ben shrugged.

"Mr Blake buried the wrong one."

"You mean—?"

"Yep. When the man opened the one they found, all it had in it was the five envelopes . . . The treasure . . ."

"One for each of us," said Toby again, grinning even wider this time.

". . . And Mr Blake said, 'Oops! It's the wrong one,' and the men looked really angry."

"So the one that's buried isn't the treasure," said Boff, getting it clear. "It's the one with all his secret papers in?"

"Yes."

"The papers he needs for Wednesday?"

"Yes."

"And it's buried with the copy of the first clue?" said Charlotte, making sure.

"Yes."

"And Mr Blake says we need the first clue to find it!" Boff groaned.

"That means we still need Cedric," he said. "Cedric's got the first clue. For some reason I can't fathom, he didn't want to read it to me when I rang – said he'd call back. And when he did it was something he'd made up."

"And now the phone's cut off," said Jayne.

"Yes," said Boff. "So if he changes his mind . . . Well, I said he could post it. But let's hope the engineer fixes the phone tomorrow."

Then Charlotte explained to Ben that they had decided to become nocturnal.

"If we look for clues at night, and sleep during the day, there's less chance of being discovered by the enemy," she explained.

The idea appealed to Ben.

"Let's start now!" he said. "It's gone midnight. I saw the car leaving Blake Island, so no one's there to see us."

"Hooray!" cheered Toby. "Let's start with some hot food!"

"We should light the fire away from the tree-house," suggested Charlotte. "Then if we have to leave it suddenly, the men won't find the tree-house next to it."

The others agreed that this was a sensible idea. The woods were deliciously dark, but with their torches they found a flat piece of ground about forty metres away from the Naitabal hut. Soon they had moved the wood-pile and got a good fire burning. They realized it was risky, but they felt sure the men wouldn't come looking that night, and anyway they would hear the car first. They were all hungry and excited, and half an hour later

145

they were enjoying their first hot meal since breakfast.

But there was no time for lying around the fire holding bloated stomachs and groaning. It was almost one o'clock in the morning, and they had to find the briefcase.

"Couldn't Mr Blake remember where he buried it?" said Jayne.

"No," said Ben. "He said it was too complicated."

All traces of the fire and food were cleared away, and they climbed back inside the Naitabal hut to study the last clue they had found.

> *Where the Virginia creeper climbs,*
> *Above the cloud the silver lines,*
> *Travel where the compass points,*
> *See the stone the stream anoints.*

"Does anyone know what a Virginia creeper looks like?" said Boff.

"Yes," said Charlotte. "It's one of those things that looks a bit like ivy but goes bright red in the autumn."

"We can't wait till autumn," said Toby.

"Has anyone seen one round here?"

"There's one on Blake Island," said Charlotte, "climbing up Darkwood House."

No one needed any more prompting. They closed up the Naitabal hut, concealed the bamboo pole, and set off towards Blake Island in the darkness.

A thorough search of the reachable parts of the Virginia creeper that covered the west wall of the house produced nothing.

"The creeper goes round that window," said Charlotte. "Perhaps it's in the room inside."

This sounded sensible, so they trooped round to the unlocked front window which, luckily, the men hadn't

146

discovered. When they shone their torches round in the drawing room, the Naitabals could see that the men had been at work. Everything that could be opened had been opened, and everything that could be taken out of drawers and cupboards had been taken out and left on the floor.

"Don't switch any lights on, anyone," said Ben. "You can see this house from where the men are. If they get up in the night they might think it's funny and come over."

"That's easy," said Charlotte. She reached behind the long, thick curtains and pulled at a white knob on a panel in the right side of the deep-set window. To the others' amazement she opened it like a door, unfolded it on hinges, then closed it half across the window. She did the same with the panel above it, then with two more on the left hand side. She lifted a metal bar and the four panels were locked across the window. "Put up the shutters!" she announced proudly, standing back.

The other Naitabals were deeply impressed, particularly Ben.

"That reminds me!" he said.

"What does?"

"Those shutters. When I was in the room with Mr Blake, there were shutters across his window and they were padlocked. But when I escaped and looked up at the house, he was standing with the shutters half open."

"Perhaps the padlock wasn't locked properly," said Charlotte. "I shouldn't worry about it."

Ben brushed the worry aside.

"No, I suppose not."

They spent the next ten minutes discovering that there were shutters on every window in the house. They put them up, drawing the thick curtains across.

147

"Burglar proof!" said Charlotte. "Now we can put lights on!"

When the house was lit up, the Naitabals felt much more secure. Outside, it would still be dark and mysterious, but inside it was warm and friendly – apart from the sad sight of Mr Blake's belongings strewn everywhere.

"Those horrible men!" said Jayne, tidying some of the clothes back into drawers. "They ought to be locked up."

They were all upstairs now, near the biggest bedroom at the front of the house, which had a window facing west as well.

"This is the one the Virginia creeper goes round," said Charlotte.

They stood in the doorway, looking.

"Well!" said Charlotte. "It looks as if the men have done all the searching already! If there's any clue in here they would have found it."

"They wouldn't have bothered with a piece of paper," said Jayne. "They'd've just thrown it away."

Now Toby started tidying things up. The others joined in, lifting the mattresses back on the beds, folding the spare blankets and putting them back in the wardrobes, and closing the drawers of the chest. Except Boff. Boff wasn't helping. He was standing still in the doorway, staring into space, thinking. Suddenly, like a ghost, he moved through the room as if none of them existed. He stopped in front of the picture on the opposite wall.

"Boff?" said Charlotte.

He turned, pointing at the picture.

"Look!"

"What?"

"The picture!"

"Yes, Boff, it's a picture. So what?"

148

Everyone else had stopped tidying now, and they were all looking at it.

"What's it of?" said Boff.

"The countryside," said Charlotte sarcastically. "Very pretty."

"Anything else?" said Boff patiently, beginning to enjoy himself.

"A cottage," said Jayne.

"A tree," said Toby.

"Not a very *Naitabal* tree," sneered Ben.

They continued to name every object in the picture, except the one Boff was trying to show them. At last they gave up.

"OK, what is it?"

"A cloud," said Boff simply. "A cloud with a silver lining."

They all looked again. The cloud was dark and heavy, but stray beams of a silver sun were thrusting through it like white-hot swords, lighting it up inside.

" 'Where the Virginia creeper climbs, above the cloud the silver lines,' " quoted Boff. "Unless I'm much mistaken..." He lifted the picture from its hook and turned it back to front. There, taped to the back of the frame, was a single sheet of paper. Gently, he pulled it off and held it up in triumph.

"Well done, Boff!"

They patted him on the back as he replaced the picture and read the clue out loud.

> *"Split in two by my powerful force:*
> *Clocks strike twice – not I, of course,*
> *Ten paces towards the little people,*
> *Until you see the church's steeple."*

"That's easy," said Charlotte. "Lightning never strikes twice – not in the same place, so they say."

"Unless it's a lightning conductor," said Jayne. "It strikes them all the time."

"It's just a saying," said Charlotte.

"You're right, though," said Boff. "I bet it's a tree that's been split in two."

"I've seen it!" said Toby. "When I was exploring. I could find it again – easy as anything."

"The only thing that's worrying me about the last clue," said Ben, who had been doing some thinking of his own, "is that we haven't used the second half."

"What d'you mean?" said Jayne.

"Where's the last one? Boff?"

Boff took it out and laid it on the bed cover.

"Look!" said Ben. " 'Travel where the compass points, see the stone the stream anoints.' Where does that bit come in?"

Everyone thought about it, but no one could come up with an answer.

"Only that the compass points north," said Jayne. "But where are we supposed to start from? The picture of the clouds?"

Ben calculated.

"If we travel north from there we'll walk into the wardrobe," he said.

"Let's do the next clue," said Boff, ignoring him, "and see what happens. Perhaps that'll help."

They turned off all the lights in the house and opened the shutters again.

"We don't want those men to know we've been here," said Boff.

In spite of Toby's earlier confidence, it took the Naitabals two hours to find the lightning-struck tree in the dark.

By the time they saw it, the dull morning light was already creeping into Naitagonia.

The tree had lost its top half, and the lightning had split what was left of its trunk down the middle. They found the clue inside a milk bottle in a plastic bag, wedged into the base of the split. It said:

> *Fence and sheep run side by side,*
> *High up on the mountainside,*
> *Walk towards it straight and true,*
> *Until the ruins come into view.*

They all looked at it eagerly, but soon realized that it meant a climb to the uppermost limit of Naitagonia.

"It's five o'clock," announced Jayne, looking worn out, "and I'm frazzled."

Everyone else was looking worn out as well.

"I don't think we'd better do any more tonight," said Boff. "Let's go and get a good day's sleep."

There were no voices of protest, so they made their way wearily back to the Naitabal hut.

In the shadows, Annie watched.

CHAPTER SIXTEEN

Riefcase-bang

Cedric Morgan stood on a pile of bricks in Mr Elliott's front garden and gazed into the complex interior of Mr Elliott's skip. As always, the skip was full to overflowing with lumps of masonry, wood, glass and solidified half-bags of cement, as well as a plentiful supply of things that Mr Elliott's neighbours couldn't fit into their own dustbins.

He was already exhausted by the mental strain of being awake all night wondering if there was a simple way of finding the letter in the skip. There wasn't. But it was his last chance – his last chance to get the Naitabals' tree-house for a day. He wished he could remember *exactly* what it said . . . But he couldn't.

He ran an exploratory hand into the corners of the skip, where he thought Harry might have dropped the precious note, but he didn't expect – and didn't get – any result.

He would have to put plan B into operation. He climbed down from the pile of bricks and went to Andy Wilson's house. Andy was the fourth member of his gang (known to the Naitabals as the Igmopong). Their activities were currently suspended while their sisters were away at Guides camp.

"What d'you want?" said Andy.

Cedric led Andy to Mr Elliott's skip and stood him next to it.

"See that skip?" he said.

"Yeah."

"See all that stuff in it?"

"Yeah."

"I want it all out."

"You what?"

"I want everything out of the skip and put . . ." Cedric cast around, trying to find a clear space in Mr Elliott's front garden. Unfortunately, the whole garden was already more full of rubbish than the skip. ". . . Over there," he finished vaguely, waving his arms.

"OK," said Andy.

Andy started taking things out. A brick. A piece of wallpaper. A wooden slat.

Cedric watched him critically.

"You'll have to do it faster than that," he said, sitting down.

"OK," said Andy.

Five minutes passed before either of them spoke again.

"Why?" said Andy.

"Oh, yes, I forgot to tell you," said Cedric, coming out of his reverie. "I'm looking for a piece of paper—"

Andy stopped working and brightened.

"I found some paper . . ."

"No, not wallpaper, Andy. It's a piece of writing paper, and it's got a sort of poem thing on it. Something about a taxi. You'll know it if you see it. And if you do see it, we'll be able to spend a day in the silly old Naitabals' tree-house."

"That's good."

Cedric calculated that at Andy's present work rate, Andy was not going to empty the skip until the year 2045.

Reluctantly, Cedric wandered over and started helping.

At eleven o'clock, Mr Elliot's van drew up. Mr Elliott saw two hot boys unloading his skip, and one of them was his no-love-lost next-door neighbour, the slimy Morgan boy.

"What do you think you're doing?" he demanded.

"We were just looking for something—" began Cedric.

"Well, you can just start unlooking," interrupted Mr Elliott, wasting no time. "I want all that stuff back in there – now! The lorry's coming to empty it in the morning."

Then Mr Elliott disappeared into his house in a cloud of plaster dust, leaving the two Igmopong staring open-mouthed at his slammed front door.

Cedric began to realize that the task was hopeless, but decided to ignore Mr Elliott. With dogged determination (and Andy's blind obedience) he continued to empty the skip.

"If I ever get my hands on that Harry . . ." Cedric muttered at intervals, but the sentence was always left unfinished.

As they approached the bottom, Harry himself appeared on the pavement, keeping a safe distance from Cedric.

"Can you remember exactly *where* you threw that letter?" said Cedric belligerently. It looked as if Harry was still armed with two dead bees, so any stronger challenge was unwise at the moment.

Harry burst into a chuckle and coiled himself like a spring, ready for instant flight.

"Di'n't *really* throw it in the skip," he shouted, and ran like the wind to the safety of his own house.

*

The Naitabals had not been asleep for many hours when they awoke to the sound of voices in the woods.

"It's the men!" whispered Ben.

They lay still in the near-darkness of the Naitabal hut wondering if they'd left anything outside that might give them away.

"What time is it?" whispered Jayne.

"Eleven thirty."

The voices receded into the distance for a while, then came back. There were three voices, all different. It sounded as if they had spread out, and were systematically combing the wood. After that there was silence again for a while, apart from snatches of bird-song. Later, the bird-song changed to the alarm calls of blackbirds and blue tits and a voice, clear in the cool air, suddenly called nearby: "Traces of a fire here."

"They've found it!" whispered Charlotte. "Good job we moved it!"

"Sshhh!" said Boff.

The three voices converged around where the fire had been and there were murmurings and mumblings that the Naitabals couldn't make out. They held their breath as footsteps came clumping through the undergrowth and beneath their tree.

"They've definitely been round here," came Blondie's voice from almost under them. "Look – the brambles have been trampled, and there's more broken twigs here than usual."

"Well, they've been here," said Flymo, "but they ain't here now."

"Probably moved camp when the escaped kid came back."

"I said we should have come earlier."

"Come on, there's bound to be a tent somewhere. Perhaps they're right up on the top."

Feet crashed through the undergrowth again and the voices faded into the distance.

"They were right underneath and they didn't see us," said Jayne, breathing at last, "thanks to Charlotte and Toby's brilliant camouflage!"

"Now you know how important Mr Blake's briefcase is," said Ben. "They couldn't find it in the house, and now they think we've got it."

"Well, we haven't," said Toby, yawning, "and I'm still tired."

"So am I," said Boff, "but we'd better not sleep while the men are in the woods. One of us might start snoring."

"Or breathing like a dragon," said Jayne, looking accusingly at Ben.

Ben grinned.

"Hark at you! You snort!"

"I don't!"

"You do!"

"Do I snort, Charlotte?"

Charlotte coughed politely.

"Well—"

'Thanks!" said Jayne.

"OK, OK," said Boff. "Quiet now."

They heard no more from the men after that, and one by one they drifted into sleep.

Ben woke up at about nine o'clock in the evening, feeling hungry, and within half an hour all the others were awake. They whispered until dark, then set about getting breakfast.

The night followed a similar pattern to the previous one at first. They found the next clue wrapped round a fence post on the northern tip of Naitagonia.

"That confirms it," said Boff. "We only need the first two lines of each clue to find the next. The second two lines must be instructions to lead us to where the briefcase is buried."

"I said that ages ago," said Ben.

"What?"

"That the clues might be in two parts."

By dawn they had found all the clues. They went back to the Naitabal hut, cooked early morning dinner, and sat down to study the sum of what they had found. Boff wrote out the second halves of the clues on a single sheet of paper. They looked like a poem, with the first verse missing:

1. ?
   ?
2. *Travel where the compass points,*
   See the stone the stream anoints.
3. *Ten paces towards the little people,*
   Until you see the church's steeple.
4. *Walk towards it straight and true,*
   Until the ruins come into view.
5. *Walk due north where the water races,*
   Follow it up for twenty paces.
6. *Take three trunks of equal measure,*
   Dig, dig, dig and find your treasure!

"Travel where the compass points," said Ben, "—that means we've got to go north."

"Yes," said Charlotte. "But where from? We're sunk without the first clue."

Boff, who had been preoccupied, suddenly got up.

"There's just a chance that Cedric might have sent it

if he couldn't get through on the phone," he said. "I'm going down to check."

"I'll come with you," said Toby, feeling confident, "and get a spade from Mr Blake's outbuildings."

As they set off, the others were already poring over the verses.

"Can't we just go north until we find a stream," suggested Jayne, looking at verse two, "and follow it until we find a stone?"

"There are half a dozen streams," said Ben, "and they've all got dozens of stones in them."

"We could try one," said Charlotte. "It'll be fun, anyway, while we're waiting for Boff and Toby."

Ben fetched a compass and they set out north from the Naitabal hut, travelling as near as they could in a straight line. After several hundred metres they came to a stream.

"There!" said Ben, pointing. "There's a stone being anointed."

"Yes," said Charlotte. "And there's another, and another."

"Anyway," said Jayne, "walk west (that's where the little people live, in Ireland, isn't it?) until we see the steeple."

They walked west for a long way, and gave up when they realized there was little chance of seeing the distant church, which was way behind them to the south.

"Come on," said Charlotte, turning round. "Boff and Toby will be back by now."

Sure enough, they were waiting at the Naitabal hut, Toby armed with a large spade, and Boff looking disappointed.

"There *was* a letter," he said to Charlotte, "but it's for you." He handed her an envelope.

"It's from my mum," said Charlotte, taking it and looking at the handwriting. "I don't know why she's written – I hope nothing's wrong." She ripped open the envelope and pulled out two pieces of paper. The first was clean and new, and the second had been screwed up and straightened out again. She read the first one out loud.

"Dear Charlotte," she began. Her voice started trembling and getting louder with excitement as she read the words. "Harry insisted that I should send the enclosed. He says he tricked it from Cedric. I don't know what it all means, but he was adamant. Hope you're having a great time. Love, Mum."

Jayne squealed, "It's the clue!", Ben shouted, "*Yes!*", Toby laughed his funny silent laugh, and Boff started to look happier than he'd been a few seconds before and said, "That's why Cedric was acting so oddly! Good old Harry!"

Charlotte grappled with the second sheet and read: "*Take the taxi to the gate, ring the bell, stand and wait . . .* "

"Yes, we did that!" said Ben. "What about the bit we really need?"

"*From the place where Elliott miaowed,*" Charlotte read, "*East to the tree that touches a cloud.*"

"That's our first verse!" said Boff.

"Must be a tall tree!" said Jayne. "Come on!"

Four of them started moving east rapidly, towards where they'd made the fire, until Boff's voice came swooping down on them like a wet blanket.

"It's half-past six," he said. "We can't do it now. The men could get here at any time."

Everyone stopped and turned in a group towards him.

"Come on, Boff!" said Ben. "They aren't even out of bed yet!"

"No," agreed Jayne. "They didn't turn up until eleven o'clock yesterday."

"And they've already searched the wood and found nothing," said Charlotte, "so they won't bother us again."

"Yes," said Toby, anxious to use the spade, "but the conference is tomorrow. If we don't find the briefcase now, we won't have time to rescue Mr Blake."

Boff realized that time was against them.

"OK," he said, and followed on, but he wasn't happy.

"We're looking for a tall tree," said Jayne, running.

"They're all tall," said Ben, not very helpfully.

"Yes, but there must be a specially tall one, mustn't there, if it's got to touch a cloud?"

"I suppose so."

They reached the eastern edge of Naitagonia (a high barbed-wire fence) without noticing any specially tall trees. They retraced their steps to the Naitabal hut and tried again, and all the time Boff was checking his watch and telling them to keep their voices down.

It was sharp-eyed Jayne who noticed it.

"Look!" She pointed, and all eyes stared into the canopy.

Near the top of one of the trees in front of them was a huge, white, misty mass of flowers.

"I don't know what it is," said Jayne. "A parasitic plant, I suppose, like mistletoe – but it looks like a cloud, doesn't it?"

The others agreed that it did look like a cloud, so they obeyed verse two by walking north from its trunk, following Ben with the pocket compass. A few minutes later they reached a stream, and in the middle of the stream was a large rock with water flowing over and around it.

"That's it!" said Charlotte. "The stone being anointed.

160

Now west to the land of the little people."

"The leprechauns," explained Ben.

Every few minutes Boff shushed them, thinking he'd heard voices or twigs cracking, but none of the others heard anything.

"Probably squirrels," Jayne whispered. "Or badgers."

Her words did little to ease Boff's edginess and he lagged behind, turning as he walked, watching and listening.

By seven o'clock they had completed all but the last verse. They were standing on a bank in a remote part of the wood with the stream to their left. To their right was a clearing with three large trees evenly spaced around it. A thick layer of leaf-mould covered the ground.

"What does it say?" said Charlotte.

" 'Take three trunks of equal measure . . .' " Ben read.

". . . And 'Dig, dig, dig and find your treasure'!" said Toby, waving the spade.

"There's the three trunks," said Charlotte, "all the same size. But where do we dig?"

"In the middle," said Boff, still looking round. "Perhaps equal measure means the same distance from each trunk."

But before anyone started measuring anything, Toby saw it. It was sticking out of the ground in the exact middle of the clearing. It looked like a mobile telephone aerial, black and blunt.

"There's something – over there!" he shouted.

Everyone rushed to it and started scooping the leaf-mould away with their hands. It was obvious that the soil had only recently been disturbed. Toby came in with the spade, then. He started easing the loose soil from around the aerial and digging down deep, heaping the earth at the side. Not very far down, the spade made a hollow knocking sound and the edge of a plastic bag appeared.

They could hardly contain their excitement as the last spadeful of earth was thrown aside and eager hands reached into the hole. Boff's worries were forgotten as soon as they lifted it out. It was the briefcase, wrapped in the plastic bag, with the aerial attached to it sticking through.

"Got it!" said Jayne, tugging.

But the thrill was short-lived.

"*We'll take that,*" said a voice. It was a man's voice, and it came from further up the woods.

Boff hadn't been imagining things.

The Naitabals looked with horror as they saw a blond man emerge from the undergrowth with binoculars swinging round his neck. As he galloped down the slope towards them he whistled through his thumbs, loud, like a steam train's whistle. Two more men appeared, from different directions. They were the three from Devil's Island.

Jayne held the briefcase tight and ran.

CHAPTER SEVENTEEN

Onference-cang

"Head her off!" shouted Blondie to the others, but they were already too late. Jayne was younger than the other Naitabals, and slightly smaller, but she was the fastest sprinter. By the time the men changed direction, Jayne was already fifty metres away.

The other Naitabals pounded after them, with Blondie in hot pursuit.

"If we don't get that briefcase, you'll never see Mr Blake again!" shouted Blondie.

Jayne heard the shout, but didn't hear what it said. She flew on, clutching their precious treasure, leaping over fallen trunks and branches, skidding sideways on leafy slopes and swerving round trees and bramble patches. She knew where she was going – and she knew it was her only chance to get away from the men and hide the briefcase.

She could feel the beat of the footsteps thudding behind her. The nearest man was shouting "Give us that briefcase" and "Come back, you little devil" but the threats only made her run faster.

She was getting tired now. As she rounded a holly bush she glanced behind and realized that Flymo was catching up with her. Would she get there in time? Then, with a great thumping thrill of excitement, she saw it at last, just ahead of her. It was the Death Slide, and it was primed for action. She made a flying leap for it, grabbing the strap with her free hand, screaming the air from her lungs as she surged down the rope at frightening speed. Behind her, the man had skidded to a halt at the vertical drop, cursing. Now he would have to go round the long way. She tumbled off at the bottom and swung on to the next pulley, hurtling down again, and straight away on to the third. She jumped off and still ran on. Flymo was so far behind her, he was out of sight. She could hear the echoes of shouted instructions, useless in the distance.

Two minutes later she was at the front of the house on Blake Island. The men's car was there. She didn't know what made her think of it, but she flung open the door. She saw their mobile telephone and wrenched it off its holder. To her amazement, she saw the other black briefcase on the back seat. She grabbed that as well and disappeared into the shrubbery. She ripped open the plastic bag, tipped out the briefcase, and replaced it with the one from the car. She hid the important one in leaves under a thick shrub where they'd never find it.

At last she heard the footsteps pounding down the path from Naitagonia on to Blake Island. She scurried fifty metres through the shrubbery, and gave the mobile telephone to a garden gnome, who ignored it and carried on fishing. She ran out, making for Naitagonia on the far side of the house. Blondie was coming down that way, so she turned like a hare and ran back. By now the third man was converging on her. In different places she could see Naitabals emerging, but there was no escape. With a last defiant gesture she hurled the briefcase in its plastic bag as high as she could. It landed in the upper branches of a huge rhododendron. She ran.

Moments later she realized that the men were clambering to recover the briefcase, no longer interested in the Naitabals. She ran back, seized the mobile telephone from the gnome, darted across the drive, and disappeared into Naitagonia.

Charlotte, Boff, Ben and Toby were all in different places, running this way and that, half exhausted.

"*Aitabal-ning ree-tong!*" shouted Jayne.

Minutes later they converged together further up in the woods. Jayne triumphantly produced the mobile telephone as they hurried towards the Naitabal hut. Even as she started dialling nine-nine-nine, they heard the sound of the car roaring down to the gates. When the emergency call was answered, Jayne was relieved – and surprised – to find their story taken seriously at last, with no laughing policeman.

The others, still unaware of Jayne's clever briefcase switch, were feeling sad, deflated and weary after their night's work. But as soon as they were locked safely inside the tree-house, drinking lemonade and listening to Jayne's story, their spirits revived. Jayne told them everything – except about switching the briefcase.

"Getting their mobile phone was brilliant!" said Ben, when Jayne had finished. "The police have probably rescued Mr Blake by now."

"But we failed!" groaned Charlotte. "We lost the briefcase! Mr Blake might have been rescued, but we've lost his invention and everything!"

Jayne's moment of glory had arrived. They were all lying in their sleeping-bags by this time, bathed in the light of a single Naitabal torch.

"*But we didn't fail!*" she hissed quietly.

The others stirred on to their elbows and saw her bright eyes shining in the dim light.

"Of course we didn't fail," said Boff. "You called the

police. Keeping the briefcase would have been a bonus, but they'll see to that."

"*No, they won't!*" said Jayne, enjoying herself.

"What do you mean?"

"Why won't they?" said Charlotte.

"*The men left the first briefcase in the car! They think they've still got the one we dug up. But they haven't. I switched it for the one in the car.*"

In spite of their growing tiredness, they made the journey to retrieve the briefcase. They weren't sure if they should open it, and it was a long time before they went to sleep after that. But when their excitement finally drifted into deep sleep, none of them could have guessed that another sequence of surprising events was about to begin.

The Naitabals slept through Tuesday and most of Tuesday night. When they finally woke up, early on Wednesday morning, they were shocked to find a policeman and policewoman standing below their tree-house, on guard.

As they opened the hatch, the man said, "We've been asked to escort you and the briefcase to the Cardiff conference. When you're ready."

"Have you found Mr Blake?" said Charlotte.

"Have you caught the men?" said Ben.

"How did you know where to find us?" said Jayne.

"How do you know about the briefcase?" said Boff.

"What about breakfast?" said Toby.

"There's plenty of time, sir. When you're ready. I'm sure your questions will be answered soon enough." The policeman sniffed the air. "You, er – you might like to freshen up down at the house and put a change of clothes on," he added tactfully.

The Naitabals noticed for the first time that they had truly become part of the woods. None of them had washed much, and none of them had changed their clothes much since their arrival.

Two hours later, they were clean, changed, breakfasted – and bewildered. They were soon inside a police four-wheel-drive, the policewoman at the wheel, speeding towards Cardiff. But none of them really understood what was happening.

"Can't you tell us *any*thing?" Charlotte repeated for the twenty-third time.

"We were just given instructions to take you and the briefcase to Cardiff," repeated the policeman, for the twenty-third time as well. "We weren't told anything else."

"But is Mr Blake there? How did you know where the tree-house was? Where are the men? What's in the briefcase?"

The questions still came thick and fast, and the answers were thin and slow. Neither of the police officers knew anything.

"Did anyone say we couldn't open the briefcase?" said Ben suddenly.

"No," said the driver, turning to her companion. "They just said bring it."

"It's got combination locks," said Boff to the others. "We couldn't open it if we tried."

"Yes, we can," said Ben, suddenly remembering. "If you know what a prime number is."

"Of course I know what a prime number is. It's a number that can only be divided by itself and 'one'. How does that help?"

"Mr Blake said the combination was . . ." Ben screwed

his face in concentration, "...the only two squares of prime numbers with an 'eight' in."

Even the two police officers in the front looked baffled at this one, but Boff pulled out paper and pencil and started to scribble.

"There are three digits on each lock," he said. "That means eleven is the lowest prime number we can square ..."

Everyone looked totally mystified as Boff wrote:

$$11 \times 11 = 121$$
$$13 \times 13 = 169$$
$$17 \times 17 = 289$$
$$19 \times 19 = 361$$
$$23 \times 23 = 529$$
$$29 \times 29 = 841$$
$$31 \times 31 = 961$$

"And 'thirty-seven' is too big," Boff murmured. The only two answers with 'eight' in are the numbers two-eight-nine and eight-four-one."

Ben rotated the dials and to everyone's surprise the locks sprang open.

"That's incredible, Boff!"

"Well remembered, Ben!"

Boff lifted the lid of the case wide for everyone to see. On top was a newspaper cutting. It was headed "GOODBYE BURGLARS" and Boff read it out:

"Charles Blake (Security) Ltd claims to have invented a device that will virtually make burglaries a thing of the past. Using high-tech electronics in a small black box, the idea will become so cheap that no home will want to be without one. Manufacturing will begin as soon as hand-

built prototypes have been thoroughly tested in the field.
Charles Blake, the inventor of the box of tricks, is keeping
the exact nature of the device a closely guarded secret until
he launches it at the National Police Conference in Cardiff
next Wednesday. He has not even dared to apply for pat-
ents yet, as he wants no chance of leaks reaching his
competitors – or organized crime – until field trials are
fully completed. Mr Blake was quoted as saying, 'If you
tell anyone anything, you haven't got security.' "

"Sounds interesting!" said the police driver. "What else
have you got in there?"

"Just a small black box . . ." said Boff. "Connected to
the aerial . . ."

The Naitabals were intrigued, Boff more than any of
them. He turned the black box in his hands, found two
clips and pressed them. It sprang open and revealed a
smaller box with a videotape inside, several circuit boards
and batteries. Everyone had a good look at it, but no
one could explain it.

It was a long journey to Cardiff, and Boff was quiet
for a long, long time. But inside, his mind was generating
heat like a microwave oven. Half an hour later, he turned
to Ben.

"You said you saw Mr Blake standing with the shutters
open, didn't you?" he said.

"Yes," said Ben. "It must have been Mr Blake. It was
his room. I locked Ned in, and the other men had gone."

"But the shutter was padlocked when they took you
to see him?"

"Yes . . ."

Boff smiled a long, slow, grinning sort of smile.

"He thinks he's tricked us," he said.

Suddenly, everyone's attention was on Boff, including the two police officers in the front.

"Look out!" said Jayne. "He's on to something!"

"A few things haven't made sense," said Boff. He turned to Ben again. "Did you say Mr Blake said he'd buried the wrong case by mistake?"

"Yes," said Ben.

"*But he couldn't have.*"

"Why not?"

"Because this case was buried with the aerial sticking out of the ground, connected to the black box. *The other case didn't have an aerial* – why should it, if there were just five envelopes inside? *That means he must have known which one he was burying!*"

The others were intrigued.

"And where's the copy of the first clue?" Boff went on. "Mr Blake said it was buried in this briefcase, but it isn't! Do you know why? *Because he didn't want to give it to us!*"

"But he posted it to us!" said Charlotte.

"*He posted it to arrive after we'd gone,*" said Boff firmly. "He must have done."

"But why would he do that?"

"*To make the search difficult and exciting!*" said Boff. "Look! The clues were easy once we'd got them, don't you see? Don't you remember what the policeman said when I phoned and told him Mr Blake had disappeared? He said; '*Mr Blake told us, whatever happens, it's only a game'!*"

At last the other Naitabals understood. They began to remember other things – odd little things. The men not taking the briefcase when they first took Mr Blake – and happening to come back when the Naitabals were there. Annie watching them, and Jayne's report of hearing a mobile telephone at the ruins. All the houses with no one answering the door.

"Mr Blake planned everything!" finished Boff. "He wasn't really kidnapped at all!"

The police officers had listened, fascinated, to Boff's dissection, and the man said, "Blimey, mate, have you ever thought of becoming a detective? The best blokes in our CID couldn't have worked that lot out!"

Boff felt proud and elated. It was the best compliment he'd ever had.

"Thank you," he said. He turned to the Naitabals. "But we can't let Mr Blake think he fooled us, can we?" Then he added innocently to the police officers, "Would it be possible for you to help us get our own back on him?"

At the conference centre, the Naitabals were treated like VIPs. They were plied with ice cream and chocolates (which none of the hundreds of police in the audience seemed to have) and were led to five seats in the middle of the front row. They still had the briefcase.

One of the officers on the platform stood up.

"Ladies and gentlemen," he said. "Will you please welcome Mr Charles Blake of Charles Blake (Security) Ltd."

The Naitabals, still dazed, applauded with everyone else, and Mr Blake strode on to the platform. He looked round at the huge audience, gave a long smile to the Naitabals in the front row, and started to speak.

"Ladies and gentlemen. I have this morning filed patent papers on a security device that will revolutionize the security of modern homes, offices and factories. It is a great privilege to be able to announce it to your conference today, as it will affect your work in the future – I hope for the better. The device is called – yes, you've guessed it – a Blake-In."

A groan from the audience.

"What happens today when an alarm goes off? Neighbours often ignore it – especially if it has a history of faults – and even a quick police response is often too late to catch the culprit.

"My system involves three ideas. One is a silent alarm, the second is a videotape. But the third feature – and most important – *is a network of alarms linking as many as eight houses together.* And, ladies and gentlemen, it is all contained in a small black box."

Mr Blake held up a black box like the one in the briefcase that was still on Boff's lap.

"All I have to do is place one of these boxes in each of eight houses in a group. A unique set of frequencies is allocated. If an alarm goes off at one of the houses, *it tells the other seven of the alarm.* The others know which house it is – instantly. All seven neighbours can then keep watch together until the police arrive. *Meanwhile, the videotape inside is running, filming the first house.*

"Ladies and gentlemen. I had to test this device properly in the field, and I'm afraid I resorted to using some friends of mine without their knowledge" – he looked down at the Naitabals "to do it. I planted micro cameras at eight strategic locations, including the main gates of my house, five other local houses, and two in the woods behind my house. Every time someone approached any of those cameras, the videotape in all eight locations started rolling – and stopped when they had gone. At the same time, the alarm in the five houses was activated. We therefore built up a complete record of the activity of my friends, and from that we were able, with police help, to monitor the effectiveness of the equipment – and

172

the complete safety of my friends. Because, ladies and gentlemen, my friends are Naitabals. They lived wild in the woods for four days, but with their parents' prior agreement, their safety was assured at all times, supervised by the police.

"But that's not all. To prove that the system can be made tamper-proof, I buried a Blake-In in the ground, two hundred metres from the nearest site, with only the aerial showing. *That Blake-In will also have recorded the entire set of events*. To prove it, if one of my friends would like to bring the black box to the platform, I will now give you a sample of the contents of the videotape that was buried with it."

Mr Blake smiled and waved at Boff. Boff smiled at the other Naitabals, left his seat and climbed the steps. Mr Blake pushed the videotape into a machine on the desk, rewound it, and all eyes turned to the big projection screen on the stage.

"The first scene," said Mr Blake, pressing the "Play" button, "is the Naitabals arriving at the gates of my house on the first day."

The audience collapsed with laughter as the auditorium resounded with fast music, a voice saying "Come back here, you wotten wabbit!" and Elmer Fudd chasing Bugs Bunny across the screen.

It was over. The Naitabals were sitting in a private room in the conference hall, and Mr Blake was with them. They had got their own back on Mr Blake for trying to fool them, and their pride was intact. The audience had loved it, and so Mr Blake's invention had got off to a livelier start than he had hoped.

"Our first meeting earlier this year made a deep

impression on me," said Mr Blake. "I seem to remember half my time not knowing what was going on while you Naitabals ran circles round me. Well, this was supposed to be my revenge. I thought I'd run circles round you for a change, but you weren't completely fooled after all, were you?"

"No, Mr Blake!"

"But I bet you enjoyed it!"

"It was wonderful," said Charlotte.

"Can we do it again?" said Jayne.

Mr Blake stood up.

"I don't really think it could work again, do you?" he said. He put his head into the corridor outside and called, and in marched Blondie, Flymo and Ned – all dressed in police uniform.

"I thought you might like to thank the team," said Mr Blake. "All members of the Police Dramatic Society, of course."

The Naitabals grinned and shook hands with them. The three men seemed much nicer than when the Naitabals had last encountered them, and Ned didn't seem at all stupid.

"You caught us in the end!" said Blondie, not in a northern accent. "Mr Blake promised us a bonus if *we* brought the right briefcase to Cardiff!"

They went out, then a smart woman came in, dressed in everyday, normal sort of clothes, and carrying a black briefcase. The faded yellow hair gave her away: it was Annie of the ruins.

Mr Blake stepped forward and put his arm around her.

"And this is *Mrs* Blake," he said, beaming.

The Naitabals, already drunk with surprises, reeled yet again. Staring, they shook hands.

"Mr Blake, you *lied* to us!" said Charlotte, chiding

him. "Mrs Blake wasn't away with your family at all!"

"Of course not!" laughed Mr Blake. "She was there to keep a close eye on you – our first line of help in any emergency."

"I've never walked through so many brambles or hid behind so many trees in my life!" said Mrs Blake, laughing. "And those ruins were draughty!"

"But that isn't the end of my reward, of course," went on Mr Blake. His wife then opened the briefcase and produced five heavy envelopes. Mr Blake handed them round, one each for Charlotte, Jayne, Boff, Ben and Toby. "You may as well open them together," he added.

There were sounds of frantic ripping, followed by yet another stunned silence. The silence ended with a scream from Jayne.

"*My passport!*"

"*And tickets to Disneyland, Florida!*" screamed Charlotte.

Toby held up his passport, grinning.

"I've never had a passport before," he said. "It's my first one!"

Boff looked at him.

"Our crafty parents!" he said. "*That's why you had your photo taken, Toby!* The rest of us didn't because we already had passports!"

"This is wonderful, Mr Blake!" said Charlotte. "Are we *really* going to Florida?"

"Your flight leaves Cardiff airport in two hours' time," said Mrs Blake, as Mr Blake slipped out of the door. "We'll be coming with you, of course."

"Do our parents know?"

"Oh yes. That's why Charles had the big meeting with them – we had to assure them of your safety in the woods and, of course, arrange the trip to America."

"Where's Mr Blake gone?" said Jayne. "I want to give him a big hug."

Mrs Blake put her head out into the corridor.

"He seems to have disappeared," she said.

"Oh no!" groaned the Naitabals. "Not again!"